AS GRIMOIRE AS IT GETS

WITCHING HOUR: BOOK 5

CHRISTINE ZANE THOMAS

Copyright © 2021 by Christine Zane Thomas

All rights reserved.

The cover was designed by William Davis with Deposit Photo stock.

This is a work of fiction. Similarities to real people, places, or events are entirely coincidental.

No part of this book may be reproduced in any form or by any electronic or mechanical means, including information storage and retrieval systems, without written permission from the author, except for the use of brief quotations in a book review.

1

IN WITCH WE TALK TRUST

There had only ever been one man—one person—who I trusted absolutely. I trusted him without any doubt. If he said he was going to do something, he'd do it. If I asked him to keep a secret, that secret would never leave his lips.

He was a good man. The best, really. He was my father. He raised me. He was a constant presence throughout my life.

He was my rock.

Unfortunately, he wasn't the only man I'd trusted. Over the years, I'd given several men the benefit of the doubt—friends, boyfriends, coworkers, and husbands. Multiple.

I gave my ex-husband, Mark, an inch, and he took miles. Thousands of miles, in fact. When I caught him cheating, I fled from our home in California to my grandmother's front step in Creel Creek, Virginia.

I'd never lived in a small town before. To me, it was strange in many ways. And Creel Creek was smaller and stranger than most.

Downtown was a ghost town except for a used bookstore and smoke shop. There was a lack of dining options and hardly any night life whatsoever.

Well, that part isn't exactly true—a certain sort gathers under the moonlight once or twice every month.

Other things bothered me too. Like how the fog rolled in every morning.

Things only got weirder.

I'd been in town a few weeks when Gran dropped several truth bombs—she told me I was a witch, like her, and like my mother. She told me my powers would come in when I turned forty. That's forty as in the big four zero. I turned forty-one the other day.

And those weren't anything compared to the biggest bombshell Gran dropped that day.

Like my father, I'd always believed my mother had died in a plane crash when I was little. Gran told me that wasn't true. No, my mother—the witch—had gone missing after taking a job from a shadowy paranormal organization known as the Faction.

My father died before I could deliver this news to him in person. He was killed. Murdered by a demon.

The anniversary of his death, now just a week away, weighed heavily on my mind.

With him gone, I found it hard to truly give in and trust anyone. This was despite making a few great friends, having an amazing boyfriend, and gaining a familiar to call my own.

Brad had made the garage his makeshift home here at Dave's house. He wasn't welcome inside it. Dave, being a werewolf and not a witch, couldn't hear Brad's thoughts as I could. They were incommunicado. Basically, Dave saw Brad as a glorified pet, not the former angelic being he is.

Familiars are neutrals in Heaven's war against Hell. Instead of fighting on either side, they came to Earth. Through a pact with Mother Gaia—also known as Mother Earth—they became attendants to the magic spread across the Earth, helping witches and wizards and the like.

Brad wasn't your average familiar. Not a cat or a dog—or even a rodent. Brad had latched on to a memory in my mind of Rocket Raccoon from the *Guardians of the Galaxy* movies. He was hefty from too much cat food, had a long fluffy tail, and sported watery eyes behind his black mask.

The garage door was open and the light off. The raccoon was just a small shadow in the corner of the garage. His eyes glowed in the darkness.

"What are you up to?" I asked him.

A streetlamp at the end of the driveway cast shadows on the pavement. His attention was drawn to it. He kind of shrugged the way raccoons are able.

"Keeping an eye out." His voice was deep and gravelly. It came from nowhere and from everywhere.

I crossed the garage and sat on the bumper of Dave's minivan. I stared out at the same piece of landscape—a greenspace with sidewalk where several months ago a paranormal hunter had tried to eliminate me.

I couldn't see the small opening—the portal to the shadow realm—but I knew it was there. As always, I could sense its magic thrumming with power.

Somehow, Brad had ripped a hole through reality to use his magic to stop the hunter. Familiars can't use magic in this realm, on Earth. Brad had exploited a technicality. He'd been in the shadow realm at the time.

"I'm guessing you haven't seen much activity lately." It was more a question than an actual guess.

He answered, "All quiet on the western front."

I half smiled at the joke. "But you're worried. I can see you're worried."

"Of course I am. Aren't you?"

I struggled a moment. I knew what this was about. I hadn't forgotten. It was just crazy how close we were to something else I'd been dreading for a long time.

My father's death had been the catalyst for a chain of events, ultimately leading to my agreement to set a demon free for one hour of a day a year from that day.

And now, a year had passed.

This was how much freedom, even a short one, meant for a demon.

All immortals are bound by rules. This included the fallen, whether they became familiars or demons. Unless summoned, a demon was bound to the shadow realm and the realms connected to it.

But unlike familiars, if a demon was let loose in our world, they could use their powers.

Every minute a demon had in our world was a threat. Custos was getting sixty.

This was in exchange for two things: Brad's freedom from the prison realm. And for Custos to hold *another* prisoner.

The demon Beruth had something to do with my mother's disappearance. What that something was, well, I wasn't sure.

Around the same time, she had taken Kalene's mother captive. After years of torment, Rainbow Moone eventually captured her captor, trapping the demon with her in the shadow realm. But Beruth had wriggled free. She killed my father, and she tried to kill me.

"I'm taking it one day at a time," I told Brad. "First, I'll drink to my father's memory. Then I'll worry about the demon."

Brad made a throaty sound. "I notice you haven't trusted Dave with any of this."

There was that word again. *Trust.*

A sinking sensation took residence in my chest. "I haven't told many people about it. It's between me and you and the demon. Honestly, I thought you were helping me out with this."

"I am," Brad said defensively. "I have a plan if you're willing to hear me out. And it's between you, me, and Stevie. Plus, I think your grandmother knows something."

"She does. But I don't want her help."

"You don't want it, or you don't want to ask for it?"

"Both," I said.

"What about the Faction? Do they know?"

"They have more important things to worry about." Brad's beady eyes narrowed, but he didn't say what he was thinking.

Much unlike my readable face and thoughts, Brad's thoughts were inscrutable. I didn't have access to them. And his bandit face gave no clues, nothing aside from being adorable.

I could only guess what his thoughts were.

My friends in the Faction—the same organization responsible for my mother's disappearance—were working to help me find my mother's body.

I had some comfort, knowing her spirit was safe. She inhabited the body of a local owl. But it wasn't the same thing as having my mother back. Not even close.

For months, we'd been running on a theory that her familiar had taken her body somehow. His name was Mr.

Whiskers. I had vague memories of him from when I was a kid. And Stevie, Gran's familiar, had met him once.

Like demons, familiars have their own set of rules. They're allowed to walk freely on Earth, but their magic is limited. They can only use it in the other realms. That is, unless they find another magical source.

And I knew where a source like that used to be...

Nothing about this theory sat right.

So far, there was no sign of him or my mother's body.

I needed the Faction's help, which they offered to me if I agreed to join them. I'd waffled on the decision for months before finally relenting.

Since then, I'd hardly seen them. We barely spoke. It seemed they were no closer to solving my mother's disappearance than I'd been working on it alone.

Brad stretched in a downward dog pose. "What you do and don't tell them is your business. It's hard for you to trust them, isn't it?"

That word.

"A little."

Taking his eyes away from the invisible portal, he cocked his small furry head in my direction.

"Okay," I said. "It is. It's hard for me to trust anyone."

"Do you trust me?" His words were so familiar, as if he'd asked the same question before.

I stumbled on my answer. "I... I do."

"This is going to work," he promised. "Let me explain what we have to do."

He gave a lengthy and technical explanation of things I'd never understand about magic and the shadow realm—its strengths, pitfalls, and challenges. At least we had a plan. Better than my usual technique of winging it and hoping for the best.

I'd gotten lucky so many times.

"It wasn't all luck," Brad said, reading my thoughts.

I rolled my eyes. "It was a lot of luck."

Right now, there wasn't any room for luck.

Brad's explanation was meant to put my mind at ease; instead, it put me on edge. There were so many things that could go wrong.

Under this plan, I had to handle Custos twice. Brad wanted me to summon and bind him a week early, so he could put some sort of shadow realm trace on him ahead of time. This would enable us to find Custos should he make a run for it.

"Okay," I said. "So, when do we do this?"

"Soon," he said.

"How soon?"

"The sooner the better."

"Tomorrow then?"

"Like you read my mind." Brad's mouth opened into a smile.

"Hardy har," I said, but I wasn't smiling. "You aren't worried?"

"No. Why should I be?"

"I don't know." I shrugged. "What if you get trapped again? What if it goes wrong and he takes you back to that realm—that prison?"

"It doesn't scare me, Constance. I've been around since the dawn of time. There's no pain I haven't already endured."

"Isn't it lonely though?"

"Believe it or not, I'm used to solitude. It goes hand in hand with being a celestial being. It's this connection—our connection—that's new to me."

I nodded. "Same here. But this whole thing is risky. Is it

worth it even? Why *don't* we just let him go free? And trust him to come back. I mean, I know why, but I don't know."

"Like I've told you before, he's bound by rules. We all are. Humans and witches too. Letting him roam this world free is like taking away those rules. He won't have to come back."

"I should never have agreed to this. I should've been patient."

"And I'd still be stuck down there."

"I would've thought of something else."

"You wouldn't have."

"This is my mistake," I said. "Not yours. I agreed to it." There was a real possibility that if things went wrong, Brad would end up back in that prison. "Why should you have to sacrifice for me?"

"Our connection makes it worth it," he said. "I get forever to come back from a mistake. A simple mistake for a human can end everything."

"Stupid human problems," I huffed.

"More like stupid witch problems."

"Hey!"

"I'm not calling you stupid." His smile widened. "It's the predicament we're in."

"Predicaments," I corrected

Brad's eyes glittered in the moonlight. He went back to staring out into the darkness.

We were quiet for a few minutes.

"What was it like?" I finally asked. "Being an angel, I mean."

"Like nothing you can imagine. Nothing like the words they put in those books. Not like the images either. I can show you, if you like. Through our connection."

"You can?"

"I can. But you'd have to trust me."

"You keep saying that."

"I keep saying it," he said, "because I'm not sure you do…"

2

IN WITCH I BIND A DEMON

I hadn't exactly abandoned Gran since I moved into Dave's place. I still picked up her groceries and checked in on her every few days. We ate dinner together once a week. And on the weekends, I tended the garden where we grew magical herbs and some basil.

It wasn't much of a stretch to say things were different. The whole dynamic between us had changed. But Gran was every bit the same fiery old lady I'd moved in with when my life hit rock bottom.

Sometimes, I wondered how it could've been different. What if Mark just told me about his affair—what if he didn't have an affair at all?

Don't get me wrong. The outcome would've been much the same. I'd still be divorced.

But maybe my magic wouldn't have gone haywire like it did that day, freezing time. Maybe I wouldn't have gotten fired, spoken to a lawyer, and set out across the continent.

Gran's spell—the one that drew me here to Creel Creek —wouldn't have worked. For it to work, magic requires a great need. In that moment, I needed a change. A big one.

It granted me that and then some.

If Mark had just been a man and owned up to his shortcomings, I could've gone on living my life without knowing I was a witch. My magic might not have manifested at all.

I still had a key to Gran's house. I held it at the ready and knocked on the door politely. I fully expected Gran's drawl ordering me to use the key so she wouldn't have to get up.

Only silence greeted me from the other side of the door. I unlocked it and went inside.

From the cramped foyer, I saw Gran's recliner, empty. There wasn't a cat or her familiar, Stevie, in sight. My own familiar, Brad, was presently in the shadow realm, getting ready.

"Hello?" I called out.

It was rare for Gran to leave the house, but it wasn't outside the realm of possibility. Pigs will fly if you give them a broom.

I stood in the living room, ears pricked. There was only the sound of the house—the A/C clicking on, a ticking grandfather clock, ice cracking free from the ice maker and tumbling to the container below.

I wouldn't put it past Gran to be napping at this time of day—at any time of day.

"Gran?" I called up the stairs.

An answer came from above, a slight rumble, like the house settling. Except it wasn't accompanied by the usual shuffling of feet or scampering of paws.

Why do empty houses have to make odd sounds?

I shrugged and went about my business, gathering supplies and heading out to the garage.

Under Gran's old Buick, she kept a binding circle—a place to trap spirits or supernatural beasts. The circle itself was over five feet wide, rusted and made of iron; it was embedded in the concrete. At its center, and also in the concrete, there was a much shinier object—a silver pentagram. Runes nestled inside each of its triangular points.

I hit the entire circle with a leaf blower. Then, to reinforce the magic, I made another circle of salt just outside the iron circle.

The circles would allow me to summon and bind the demon.

He wouldn't like that. I brought some other things along to ease the blow.

I set down a half gallon of chocolate ice cream and a handle of whiskey, and not just any whiskey, but something Cyrus had suggested. Cyrus owned the local vineyard, and he happened to be the most ancient being I knew. If he said something was good, it was good.

The whiskey cost me a week's paycheck. Not that my boss paid especially well.

I stepped carefully over the salt line, took my place across from the right rune, and began to summon.

"Hear my voice through Shadow Realm to the depths of Nether,
hear it deep in the worlds they call Never Nether.
Hear me summon the Jailer of Spirits,
I summon Hell's own demon guard,
Custos the Conniving I summon you now,
here, appear in my wards."

Black smoke began to billow from the circle. It stopped at the salt line and spiraled into the air, creating a cylinder of thick smoke.

"And by the laws of our ancient craft, I bind thee to this circle.
I bind thee and seek counsel.
I bind thee."

"Yes. Yes. You bind thee," said a nasally voice from inside the smoke. The smoke cleared from the room in a single puff, revealing the demon.

Like a mime, he tested the iron border. He stuck a hand toward it and found something solid. He wasn't trying to force his way out. Not yet. But I jerked back anyway. His light touch sent a small jolt of pain through me.

The last time this circle was used, I had Gran and Hilda Jefferies here with me, their magic strengthening the binding.

Now, it was just me—me being foolish. I wasn't so sure I was strong enough to keep the demon inside should he try and force his way out. If there was any flaw in the circle or in the circle of my mind, he could find and exploit it.

I straightened. It wasn't a good time to show weakness.

The demon grinned.

Custos bore the appearance of a man in the same manner a wolf can look like a dog from far away. Closer, you see the size of the teeth. His eyes were crimson red, and not just the iris. There was no white. No pupil. His teeth were the opposite. Too white. Too sharp. He wore a suit, tailored to fit his frame, which appeared average.

Behind him, something was hidden under the suit's jacket. *Wings, maybe?*

Custos bent down and helped himself to the whiskey with an eager hand. He didn't bother removing the cork. He jerked his wrist to break the glass, leaving a jagged opening he put to his lips without any hesitation.

After several long pulls, he set the bottle down and used the same enthusiasm to open the ice cream. Before digging in, he saluted me with the plastic spoon I'd left there for him.

"You're a little early and—" he used the spoon to indicate the binding circle "—I don't believe this was part of our deal."

"You're right." I nodded. "It wasn't."

He sighed and dug out a big scoop. He took more care with the plastic spoon than he had the glass, relishing the cold treat and licking the spoon clean with a forked tongue. "I know what this is about."

"You're wrong." I shook my head. "I'm still honoring our deal. As promised."

"You are?" He raked his nails against the barrier. "Could've fooled me."

A hiss of pain made my teeth clench. "Let me explain."

"It's not as if I have anywhere else I can go."

"It won't be today," I said. "But on the anniversary of our deal. You have my word."

"Oh, I've had your word for some time. And your demon. You do understand what will happen should our contract be broken?"

"I do understand. Or I think I do."

"And we're not adding more terms. A deal is a deal."

"I'm not adding more terms," I said. "But I'm unsure about something."

He arched an eyebrow.

"What happens while you're gone? Who takes over? Could the demon—could Beruth escape?"

He scooped up the whiskey. "My safeguards can stand up to anything. To anyone. At least for a short while. It's an hour. What's the worst that could happen?"

"You tell me," I said. "What would happen if Beruth got free from your realm?"

He shrugged. "Nothing much. She's still a demon. Still bound to the shadow realm unless someone calls her elsewhere."

"Elsewhere meaning here—to Earth?"

He bent his head in a slight nod and rolled his red eyes, acting as if I was asking the dumbest questions he'd ever heard.

Maybe I was. "Okay... what's stopping someone from summoning her now?"

"My realm," he said, then drained the whiskey. "I am the only entity who can be summoned from it. You know for yourself that's true. Did you not try to summon your familiar?"

"I tried."

Custos narrowed his crimson eyes. "Where is the little scamp?"

He's on his way, Brad's thoughts echoed in my head.

Done? I asked.

It took longer than I thought it would. But yes.

The demon looked around the garage, suspicion growing and lines forming on his brow.

I nodded to myself. I had to give Brad some time. "You know as well as I do he isn't a scamp."

"I'm sorry if I find it funny—to choose such a demeaning life. I like that word: demeaning. It serves them well. Familiars aren't so different from demons. It stems from the same choice, after all. We both sin. Now, where is he?"

"I'm here." Brad appeared from the kitchen. How he managed to nudge the door open, I didn't know.

"Hello again," Custos said.

"Hello, jailer." Brad stayed well away from the circle's

boundary. It was hard to see emotion in his raccoon face, and yet, somehow the wariness in his dark eyes shone through.

"It wasn't my fault. Blame the spell. Blame the caster. I can't help if I was compelled to lock you in my prison."

It might've been my mind playing a trick on me, but for a second, in my peripheral vision, Brad's form flickered from raccoon to something else. Something angelic.

They might've made similar decisions, but the paths they took were different. Custos's path turned him into a monster. In the shadow realm, Brad reverted to his true form. He was like a marble statue. Chiseled and perfect.

"Did you ever tell us who cast the spell?" Brad asked the demon. "Was it Hal?"

"The bumbling oaf?" Custos snickered. "No. No. I'm afraid he had help."

"What kind of help?" I asked.

"A woman. She looked a lot like you."

"What do you mean? She was a witch? She was blonde?"

"No. I mean she looked a lot like you. Similar features. Maybe she was a few years older. I'm afraid I don't really understand the aging thing."

"Was she *really* a woman though?" We had experienced possession of bodies before—from a demon inside my own head to a familiar occupying Gran's neighbor Agatha.

"That's an interesting question." The demon licked his lips with his forked tongue. "What do I get out of this if I answer it?"

"What do you mean?"

"I mean what do I get for offering you this information?"

"You earn our trust," Brad said.

The demon chuckled again. "Trust isn't earned by

sharing secrets. It's hard fought. It's earned by keeping promises. Something you two haven't done."

"Yet," I exclaimed.

Custos smiled an evil smile. His teeth were like daggers. "I think you two already know the answer. It was a woman in appearance only. Something else lurked underneath."

"Who?"

"I'm done answering your questions. That is, unless you wish to compel me to answer—you've bound me here, after all—you could do it. You could try."

"Don't play into his games," Brad boomed.

"I won't," I said. "And he's right. Information doesn't prove he's trustworthy. It doesn't prove anything."

3

CREEL CREEK AFTER DARK
EPISODE 106

It's getting late.
Very late.
The creeping dread of tomorrow haunts your dreams.
It's dark out. Are you afraid?
Welcome to Creel Creek After Dark.

Yeah... yeah. I'm your host Ivana Steak.

Listen. I know it's been a while. I'm sorry I haven't put an episode out in two months. It's just, well, it's been rough.

I wanted to hop on here and tell you I'm still alive... If you care, that is.

Some of you do. I've been getting your emails. Lots of emails. And I've watched your ParaTube videos too. They're awesome. Really, they are. I promise to go live there soon.

It's just, *Creel Creek After Dark* isn't the same without Athena.

I wanted to do this without her. Really, I did. I thought I was capable. But she did so much work you folks never saw. So much behind the scenes.

And that proof I hoped to find—well, it's been harder to come by than I originally thought.

Maybe that's not all my fault. Creel Creek has been especially quiet the past six months. So quiet. That's bound to change, right?

Yeah, so what does this all mean? Why am I blabbering away on here to a handful of listeners?

It's simple, really. I want to get back to normal. The paranormal. I want the podcast to get back on track.

Tell you what. Join me live on ParaTube next week for a special live recording of *Creel Creek After Dark*. I'll answer your questions. Field your calls. And we'll get back to the business at hand.

This is season two. I still want to expose the paranormal elements of this town. I know you want it too. So, let's do it together.

This is Ivana Steak saying I can't do it alone. I need your help.

4

IN WITCH DATE NIGHT IS RUINED

The reality was, Custos hadn't given us any new information. Not really. At most, he'd verified my suspicions.

But something still wasn't sitting quite right.

I wondered if my gift from Mother Gaia was fading. Did her gift have a time limit like so many others?

The Mother never actually told us what we were given that day—the day we called her and asked for her help. She'd left it for each of us to figure out.

She'd given Gran time.

It took me ages to figure it out, but I had been given something special. Confidence in my decision making.

I knew when I was right. Or wrong.

Except this new information was messing with my head.

I knew my mother's familiar, Mr. Whiskers, had played some part in her disappearance. The gift told me this was true. Only when I tried to place Mr. Whiskers into the current mix—tried to use that knowledge to find my mother's corporeal form—I came up empty.

And when I tried the same thing, putting Mr. Whiskers

with Halitosis Hal and the sending of Brad to Custos's realm, the results were nonexistent. It was like a Magic 8-Ball responding, "Reply hazy, try again."

Hazy... That's how I felt when I got home to Dave's house.

I found it suspiciously quiet. There was no sound from the girls—Dave's three daughters. I could usually count on them to be crying, laughing, or fighting. Sometimes, all three.

The TV was on at a reasonable volume. And it sounded oddly like sports.

What is going on?

I tiptoed from the garage door to the kitchen, expecting to catch Dave relaxing in his recliner. Like Gran's, it was empty.

Something wasn't right. Maybe I was forgetting something—my gift told me that much was true.

I went upstairs to our room and heard the shower running. It wasn't the only thing I heard. My handsome boyfriend had morphed into a baritone vocalist. He was belting the opening lyrics to "You've Lost That Lovin' Feelin'" by The Righteous Brothers.

It was like that scene in *Top Gun*, except a lot more naked.

"Hey!" I protested. "I still close my eyes." I squinted through the steamy bathroom, not even feigning disinterest in the blurred physique on the opposite side of the shower glass.

"Where've you been all afternoon?" He turned toward me. His thick chest hair was covered in bubbly suds.

Lying to Dave wasn't my forte. "I went to Gran's house."

"Oh yeah?"

I chose to redirect. "She wasn't there—if you can believe it?"

"Not there?" He grinned. "That's out of character."

"I know. I wonder where she was."

"I know the feeling. I was beginning to think you were going to stand me up on date night."

How could I forget about date night?

It had been an eventful day.

But still, date nights were almost as rare as Gran getting out of the house. They were like an eclipse—the Sun, the Moon, and the Earth had to be in alignment.

Like crescent moons and solstices, an eclipse was a powerful magical event. This eclipse had our local non-coven witches abuzz. Gran had never wanted to call our little get-togethers anything official, but recent events necessitated she take a backseat. We were doing things our way—me, my best friend Trish, our friend Lauren, and a few other local witches. Our bond was getting stronger with each meeting.

It wasn't just witches. There were many active paranormals in the Creel Creek community. Every month, Dave went to meetings of the League of Artemis—a national organization of shifters—who had reluctantly accepted a werewolf into their ranks.

Dave lathered his face and took a razor to it. I could swear at the end of it, there were already flecks of stubble peppering his square jaw.

We chatted as we got ready, changing into what passed for suitable going out attire for a couple in their forties in a town as small as Creel Creek.

The girls had gone with Dave's sister Imogene for the night, and he'd been alone the whole afternoon. When it became apparent I wasn't coming home early, he did some cleaning around the house. Probably why he needed a shower.

I sighed.

I'd squandered an afternoon alone with Dave just to talk to a demon—and put a trace on him. It wasn't a fair trade. But it would be all right. We had the entire night to be alone together.

I wanted to stay in, order pizza, and watch a movie that wasn't animated. Then Dave pointed out that the only change from our typical Friday routine was the movie's rating.

It was a good point.

It was how we wound up at Orange Blossoms, a chain restaurant offering oversized burgers, overcooked steaks, and overpriced drinks. We found a cramped booth near the bar, and I ordered one of those overpriced cocktails.

It tasted mostly of rum. After slurping it down, I was feeling a slight buzz.

I could do that again—get a buzz. Given another shot, I could get drunk. The gift that Hilda had gifted me on my fortieth birthday—making me impervious to poisons—had faded along with all the others.

Turning forty-one meant I was no longer a rookie witch. I had a year of witching under my belt. And the gifts I was given at my birthday ceremony were gone now.

I relished being able to catch a buzz again. Not that I was going to overdo it. I had plenty to look forward to this evening; I didn't want to fall asleep on the car ride home.

Our food was slow to arrive. Dave was almost as antsy as me. Under the table, his fingers stroked from my knee to the hem of my dress. I was about to playfully slap his hand away when his finger came to an abrupt stop.

There was a loud crunching sound outside, followed by several crashes—like windshields shattering.

We reacted at the same time.

And we were a fraction too late.

The glass doors and windows all burst at once, as if there'd been an explosion outside. Like a bomb had gone off in the parking lot.

Of the gifts I'd been given when I turned forty, I missed Gran's, in particular. The warning signs—the prickling sensation on the back of my neck and the magic flowing freely to my fingertips—they no longer kicked in at the first sign of danger.

No. They kicked in during the danger.

And they were kicking in right now.

Here, I thought I was done dealing with supernatural creatures for the day, but no such luck.

A hideous monster barreled through what was left of the front wall. It pushed through the wreckage at the front of the restaurant—the flipped over tables and broken glass. Wreckage it created barreling through the wall

I'd never seen anything like it. Not on Earth. Not in my nightmares. Not even in horror movies. Its body was a mix of slime and puss. Teeth protruded from a wide mouth like the curled tusks of a boar. The being's eyes were hidden behind narrow slits of its folded, mucus-colored flesh.

It was huge. As big as an elephant but it stood on two legs like a bear.

People were screaming, running, and hiding. Or they were, until time stood still.

Shards of glass hung in the air. My drink tipped sideways on the table, half of it already spilled, the slush frozen in midair.

I hadn't uttered the spell. I couldn't even remember thinking it. But I had reacted by doing the only thing I knew well.

And I was the only person outside the spell.

Had I been thinking clearly, I would've spelled Dave outside it too. We could've planned something. We would've figured a way out of this together.

As it was, he was as frozen as my drink, his eyes locked on the monster.

It, too, was motionless, a torn curtain hanging from its shoulder like a cape. I ventured a few steps closer, my sandals crunching on the glass.

I was afraid to touch it. I was afraid to do anything that might reset the spell and send time into motion again.

You got to do something, a small voice in the back of my mind said.

I called my magic and thought of spell after spell.

"Banish the horror to whence it came,
without what it came for, no victims to name."

Then I tried:

"Shrink it down. And keep it bound."

They weren't my best spells. But they weren't my worst either. Nothing worked. And I could feel my hold on the time spell unwinding.

I had to think fast.

I got everyone I could out of harm's way, corralling them toward the back exit.

Everyone but Dave. I patted down his pockets, finding his keys, his wallet, and his phone. Everything except what I wanted to find. The totem that allowed him to turn into his wolf form was nowhere to be found.

Sheriff Dave was just going to have to do. I stood him up beside the crowd, hoping he'd understand. He had to lead them to safety.

I, on the other hand, had to lead this thing—whatever it was—away from Orange Blossoms.

I moved around it, over the broken wall, and onto the sidewalk at the front of the restaurant.

Then, on my terms, I let go of the spell, and time ratcheted up to full speed. I sent a bolt of lightning at the beast.

Either because I made it mad or because it sensed easy prey, the beast followed me out and through the parking lot.

Cars were flipped over, and there was glass everywhere.

I was already regretting my choice of shoes before this monster showed up, now I really hated them. I ran to the street like I was John McClane in everyone's favorite not-quite-Christmas movie.

A raccoon skittered across my path, startling me, but I kept running. The thing behind me continued its charge.

"Do you trust me?" Brad asked.

That word again.

"I'm a bit busy right now. Ask me again later."

"Think happy thoughts," he said. "And run. Don't look back."

I did as he said and ran, cutting across the empty street.

Familiars have no true power on Earth. Their bodies are mere vessels. Their true power resides somewhere else. Namely, the shadow realm. There, familiars have the same or better magic than I do.

Here and now, Brad was just a raccoon who had all the

powers—or lack thereof—a raccoon possesses. He could scavenge and look cute.

I highly doubted his cuteness could help take out this nightmare beast. It roared behind us, getting closer.

"What's the plan?" I asked, short of breath.

"The plan," Brad said, "is to think happy thoughts. You aren't yet."

"Please, stop looking in my head. It isn't helping."

"Yeah, well, at least I'm trying."

I tried to think happy thoughts. I really did. But it reminded me too much of *Hook*, a movie my dad and I saw in the theater. I thought about him and all I felt was sad.

"That's better!" Brad swerved into an alley, and I followed. I quickly regretted the decision. The alley came to an end at a dumpster ahead of a solid brick wall. On one side of the dumpster, there was a staircase to the second floor of an abandoned industrial building.

"How is that better? I was thinking a sad thought."

"Happy. Sad. They both work in this situation. It's fear and anger that'll work against you."

The raccoon scampered up the steps. We were halfway up when the monster pounded to the bottom, roaring.

"Don't look back," Brad said. "Keep thinking those thoughts."

"Is that door going to open?" I panted.

"Trust me," he said again. "And keep thinking."

"You keep saying that!"

I tried to picture my dad. His smile. The way he'd pretend to get mad when I ate the last bowl of ice cream or when I stole the remote to watch a show he hated.

Maybe he was mad. Maybe not. Either way, he always bought another pint. And he always stayed in his chair, watching the show and complaining about stilted dialogue.

Brad veered sideways, directly under my feet. I lifted my foot in an attempt to miss him and missed the step entirely. I went tumbling backward, down the metal stairs.

I was still thinking about my dad, still holding on to that picture of his smile.

There was a squelching pop as I collided with something solid. It was sticky and wet.

Whatever it was, it broke my fall. I landed on the concrete beneath the stairs without breaking my neck.

I hadn't come away totally unscathed. The air was knocked out of my chest, and my elbow burned with a sudden, shooting pain. There was a ringing sensation in my ears.

I gasped for breath. When I found it, I was overwhelmed by the stinking odor of a bog.

Bleary-eyed, I searched above me and only found Brad at the top of the stairwell. "Where'd it go?"

Carefully, he padded down the stairs.

"It's on your jeans," he said. "And your shirt. Oh, and there's a lot in your hair. A big ole smudge of it on your cheek too."

"You mean it's gone?"

"It is."

"What was that?"

"A ghoul," he said. "A fractured spirit, mostly malice and rage. They only have one good rampage in them. He had to make that body out of spare parts and mud. One rampage and it's over. Your happy thoughts and gravity did the rest."

"Sad thoughts," I corrected. "Why didn't magic work?"

I struggled to get to my feet.

"You didn't know the right spell." Brad scooted around the puddles of what used to be ghoul.

"You could've told me the right spell."

"I didn't know it either. The sad thoughts worked well enough."

"So you say."

My arm was throbbing. I'd cut it on one of its tusks. There was a stream of blood running down from my elbow.

I was sticky everywhere.

There were still memories of my dad hovering inside my head.

Dave rounded the corner, looking more menacing than I would have thought possible. Without his gun or the talisman, he shouldn't be that much of a threat. Yet, something in his eyes and the tension in his jaw made me want to turn into a puddle.

His eyes went wide as he took in the scene. Then he gathered me into his arms and noticed the blood oozing from mine.

Without any thought, he unbuttoned his long-sleeved shirt and ripped off a sleeve. He tied it over my wound, then cradled me, bare-chested.

"Gross," Brad said.

"It's not gross," I argued.

"Not you. That!" He pointed.

The muck around my feet started to move. There was blood on the concrete—my blood—the muck swirled around it as if to try and build itself again.

"Do something," Brad boomed.

Dave tried to pull us away, but I was frozen, aghast at a grotesque figure—a miniature replica of the ghoul—rising from the gunk.

The little ghoul looked up at us, then spun around and darted away.

I didn't know what to do. The magic hadn't worked last time. Not really. I didn't have a spell to use.

Brad took up the mantle. He chased the thing down, pounced on it like a cat, then ripped it apart with his dexterous paws and his sharp teeth.

Or he tried to. Nothing was working.

"Are you thinking happy thoughts?" I asked.

He shook it some more. It let out a ghastly scream as it popped, spraying awful goop from Brad's jaws.

I sighed with relief. It was over. Or it seemed to be. I kicked at the carnage on the ground. It was like a dumpster of mud had exploded in the alley.

"I thought you said they only had one rampage in them?"

"Usually," he said, spitting. "It was your blood. It gave it a second life."

I scowled. "Why would it do that?"

"Magic." The raccoon began sifting through a mound of muck, found nothing, and went to another. That one yielded... something. It dangled from his mouth. Thin and metallic—it was a necklace of some sort.

Brad scurried over and handed it to me. It was simple, a chain holding a heart pendant. The heart was cut from a stone I didn't recognize. It barely reflected in the streetlights.

"Let me see that." Dave held out his hand.

"Why? Does it look familiar?"

"Not really." He pursed his lips. "But I can check around. Why do you think that thing had this?"

I shrugged.

"Magic," Brad said again. "It's faint. I think there must've been a charm on it or something. In this realm, the ghoul is nothing but a spirit. An evil spirit, but a spirit nonetheless. They need magic to build themselves a form like that. This must've supplied the power."

"Ah. Magic." I nodded, conveying the information to

Dave, who stuffed the necklace in his pocket. He normally treated evidence more respectfully.

"Come on. Let's get back to Orange Blossoms." Dave tugged me at the waist and started walking.

I didn't budge. I just couldn't take my eyes off the alley. I wanted to know more about ghóuls. I wanted to know why it had come here.

I wanted answers.

There were no answers to be had. At least not from the ghoul.

"Come on, Constance. We should get that arm looked after."

"I will. I just…"

"Go," Brad said. "There's nothing else here."

Dave tightened his grip on me, and I gave in. He maneuvered us in the direction of Orange Blossoms. "Mac should be at the scene by now. There's more than a few memories you'll need to wipe, if you're up for it."

I leaned into him. "I don't know. I'm a bit of a mess."

Like the alley, I was covered in muck. It clumped in my hair and clung to my clothes.

"We'll get you cleaned up." He looked at me, then down at the muck now caked on his side. "Correction. We'll both get cleaned up."

"I hope that means you're going to sing to me in the shower."

He shook his head, smiling, and began to sing.

5

IN WITCH THE FACTION RETURNS

Sleep wouldn't find us for another few hours. And it was just sleep. For me, it was a deep, dreamless sleep with no nightmares. No monsters.

My eyes had only been closed a minute or two when I heard something worse—the alarm on my phone.

These days, alarms aren't the bleeping, buzzing nuisances they used to be. Now, they play a favorite song or a soothing crescendo.

An alarm is still an alarm.

On a good morning, I wanted to throw my phone with its soothing melody out the proverbial window. This was *not* a good morning.

It was the other kind.

It felt like I'd blinked, and now the alarm was accosting me.

I groaned a few times. I peeked at the time through a single slit, checking if it was some mistake.

I even contemplated stopping time. But I wasn't sure the spell would allow that.

Can I sleep while the world stands still?

Does the spell even stop time at all? Or just make the things around me motionless?

It was too early for thought-provoking questions like that.

Beside me, Dave was snoring softly. I rolled over to kiss his cheek and felt a twinge of pain near my elbow—the cut, still fresh. After I'd tried to spell it better, the EMTs had given me a butterfly bandage.

Dave stirred, then put his arm around me. "Is it that time already?" His voice was scratchy and deep.

"It is, according to *some* time measurement devices. I'm open to debating it."

"You can call Trish. I'm sure she'll understand..."

He made a good suggestion. A very good one. And his side of the bed was warm, cozy, and inviting. I knew if I shut my eyes for more than a second, they'd stay shut for a whole lot longer.

"I'm fine though." I blinked. "And she's not a morning person." That was an understatement. Trish wasn't an any time of day person. Mornings just happened to be her worst.

"How is it that two non-morning people operate a coffee shop?" I could hear the smile backing Dave's question.

"Technically, it's a bookstore."

Trish was my best friend and the owner of Bewitched Books, where I'd worked for over a year. It used to be a pretty laid-back gig—starting midmorning and a few customers throughout the day. That was on days we were lucky enough to get customers.

I only had myself to blame for the changes. Coffee was my idea. The business became a joint venture—when I facilitated us getting a fancy espresso machine. We rearranged the whole store to cram a coffee bar near the front window.

It was a hit, too. The whole town came out in droves to support us. Or maybe it was their coffee addictions they were supporting. It felt like the same thing.

I got up and got dressed.

Dave went back to snoring, although I doubted he'd sleep for long. Today was supposed to be one of his days off. The ghoul business had thrown a wrench in that.

There was a lot of cleanup left to do. Orange Blossoms was still a disaster zone. Dave would have to coordinate with city officials, the county, and whoever else to get things put right.

On top of that, there'd be his least favorite part of police work—paperwork. Mountains of it, I was sure. All with the same lie. Insurance doesn't cover ghoul attacks. The claim, for now, was a gas explosion.

We could only hope that would stick. While I'd wiped as many memories as possible, there was a chance that someone had seen something they shouldn't have. Maybe even gotten a video of it to share on ParaTube or the like.

The site, along with its counterpart Creel Creek After Dark, had been rather quiet over the last few months. Then again, so had the town. This was the most action the town had seen since the craziness at the corn maze last November and its aftermath at the new year.

What a weird night.

It scared me a little—how natural it felt to get wrapped up in another mystery. If this *was* a mystery and not some isolated incident.

It didn't feel isolated.

It felt like an attack—an attack on me.

Dave would never come out and say it but being around me was dangerous.

This wasn't the first time a supernatural enemy had

surfaced and come gunning for me. Far from it. It had happened so many times now, I was beginning to lose count.

I crept out of the house a few minutes later. I was tired, but I was also eager to get out the door—eager to search for answers.

While Brad told me a few things about ghouls, I had plenty of questions left. And there was a solid chance I could find some of those answers on the shelves at Bewitched Books.

Not to mention the rodent that lived among those books. Trish's familiar Twinkie was an encyclopedia of paranormal knowledge.

Trish was no slouch either; she knew her stuff. But she wouldn't be there for hours.

Before bed, I'd blasted several text messages out to my network of magical friends. Trish included. No one had answered. Granted, I'd sent those texts late, after midnight. And it was early. There'd hardly been time in between. My body continued to remind me of that.

And Creel Creek continued to remind me it was Creel Creek. A thick fog blanketed the town. There was no sunlight, despite the sun supposedly rising.

The fog was part of the spell on the town that made it so most normal people stayed away—people without magic in their blood. Those normal folks who made homes here had trouble spotting the peculiar people surrounding them.

And speaking of peculiar, through the haze of fog, I made out three shapes loitering on the sidewalk outside the bookstore.

Customers already?

I checked the clock. I was on time. Meaning I was there thirty minutes before we were supposed to open.

Okay, more like twenty-five. But still.

I parked in the gravel behind the store, waved to the owl perched on the lamppost illuminating the back door, and unlocked that door. Then, I scrambled through the store to the front, flipping on light switches.

At the door, my hand hovered over the lock. My eyes adjusted to the light, and my heart leaped as I recognized the people on the other side of the glass.

They weren't customers.

"Look what the ghoul dragged in." I ushered them inside and relocked the bolt. "Or did you drag in the ghoul? I'm guessing you got my text?"

"I got your text." Ivan Rush nodded. "But that's not why we're here. We were already on our way."

"And the ghoul?"

"Wasn't us," Kalene Moone said. "Granted, it kind of tracks with what we've been seeing. More of the same."

"More of the same what?" I asked.

"Someone's been ushering beings from the shadow realm into this world." The third person yawned. "Sorry," he said. "I was on driving duty."

Ivan gave the taller man some room. "Constance, have you ever met Slate?"

I shook my head.

Slate Clifton was a name I'd heard spoken a few times. And I'd seen several text messages, but we hadn't met.

Slate was one of a few members Ivan had recruited to the Faction since he and Kalene left Creel Creek last year.

This counted as my third time seeing them since officially joining the Faction. In those brief encounters, Ivan and Kalene had breezed through town between crises of their own.

I hadn't met any of these recruits.

Slate was tall, at least six and half feet, and burly. He

wore wire-framed glasses too small for his large and oval face. His head was clean shaven, and he wore a bright smile when he wasn't yawning.

This man stood out in a crowd. Literally. His fist nearly touched the ceiling as he stretched his arms again.

He was the exact opposite of Ivan Rush, who looked as bland as ever—dressed mostly in dark colors. Ivan was of average height and build. He had blue-gray eyes and hair he didn't do much with, except hide it under a ball cap.

"The famous Constance Campbell." Slate's massive hand enveloped mine in a handshake. "It's a pleasure to finally meet you."

"You too, Slate. Can I get you anything? Coffee? Tea? A latte?"

"Oh. Nothing for me, thanks." He put those massive hands up, waving me off. "I'm ready to hit the hotel bed. I'll pass out for the next ten to twenty-four hours."

"You're staying at a hotel?" I don't know why that surprised me, but it did.

"The Creel Creek Mountain Lodge," Ivan said. "We're going to hole up here in Creel Creek for a while."

"You are?" I arched an eyebrow. "How long is a while?"

When I joined the Faction, I'd hoped they could help find the entity parading around in my mother's body. But they were too busy with other things—policing the paranormal community.

To be fair, I hadn't helped them do much of that either. Every time they'd asked for my help, I was busy with something—usually Dave and his girls.

"We're here as long as it takes," Kalene said.

I didn't understand what she meant.

Ivan explained, "We have reason to believe Creel Creek

is the epicenter of some activity we've been seeing. Something happened here. Recently."

My throat got very dry. When I swallowed, I could swear it echoed across the entire storefront.

There was something I'd been holding back—something big I hadn't told them.

"How recent?" I managed to ask.

"This stuff goes back years. Maybe decades."

I sighed with relief, thinking Ivan was hinting at something else.

"But this shadow realm activity really started to escalate in the past few months. You don't happen to have any ideas about that, do you, Constance?"

Or not.

Creel Creek was the epicenter.

Just outside town, near Gran's house, beneath the graveyard, there was a magical mine full of powerful rocks.

Was being the key word.

I was there when it collapsed.

How it tied in to supernatural beings escaping the shadow realm, well, that was outside my expertise.

It fell on them—the Faction. They would need the facts in order to continue their investigation.

Only I hadn't told them about the mine. I hadn't told anyone except Gran and Trish.

Summer Shields knew because she was there for it.

Even our familiars had been kept in the dark—Gran thought it could be dangerous if they knew there was a source of magic in this realm.

"I, uh—have you guys handled ghouls before?"

Slate nodded. "We've seen eight or nine the last few months alone. They aren't the only problem."

"Like what?"

"Like demons," Ivan answered, stepping ahead of Slate.

I froze, holding my breath. If I told them anything, it might put me on the Faction's top ten most wanted list.

"Constance," Ivan said, "we understand we haven't exactly held up our end of the bargain."

"If we're going to help look for your mother," Kalene said, "we need you to—"

Ivan put his hand up in Kalene's direction, not unkindly. "Kalene. We talked about this."

She nodded.

"Take your time," Ivan said to me. "It's why we're here. It's why we're here for the long haul. We need your help as much as you need ours."

Kalene acknowledged this by knitting her eyebrows together. It seemed like this was *new* information to her.

"I'll be by later this week," Ivan said. "We'll have a chat."

"Come have a drink with us tonight," Slate said. "The hotel bar has a happy hour. You know you want to come."

"You're always welcome," Ivan said.

Headlights bored into the front window as our first *real* customer pulled into an angled spot outside.

I had a lot going on that morning. Coffee to brew. Lattes to make. Books to pack. Plenty of reading up about ghouls to do.

Mostly, I had a lot to think about. It was time I decided whether I could trust the Faction.

The only problem was—I wasn't sure they could trust me.

6

IN WITCH WE'RE TRAPPED

Twinkie tried to fill some of my knowledge gaps about ghouls. Just like Brad, her experience with them was limited, but she had millennia worth of secondhand knowledge.

Like other creatures from the shadow realm, the name ghoul had been thrown around in folklore and myth for centuries. Then fictional works came along, making changes and morphing ghouls into something else—whatever the story needed.

There were plenty of books in the store that mentioned them. Almost too many. Most of them were in the fantasy section. Thanks, Jim Butcher.

While every book described ghouls a bit differently, there was one aspect that remained the same. According to the literature, ghouls fed on human flesh.

"That's not good," I told Twinkie.

We didn't have much time to dwell on that fact. Customers came out of the woodwork. Some for coffee. Most for gossip.

The rumor mill was churning in both the paranormal

and non-paranormal communities. In a town as small as Creel Creek, the coffee shop was as good a place as any to search for answers.

Some of our customers didn't pay as much attention as others. There was some paranormal talk in non-paranormal company.

I really should've wiped every mind—not just those witnesses of the muggle variety.

By the time Trish rolled into the store after nine, I was tired of hearing about it. Tired of hearing theories and fielding questions.

She even tried to interrogate me between customers, but the customers came too thick and fast, one after the other, the line sometimes growing to the doorway.

After a grunt of frustration, Trish got down to business. She was a latte making machine.

The dark haired forty-something exuded witchy energy. She looked like a stunt double from the movie *The Craft* who'd forgotten to change. She always wore a black shirt and black jeans. She was short—and not just because I'm tall—but short for anyone. She scraped past five feet by the soles on her Doc Martins. Her hair was black, except for a streak of purple in her bangs, which matched her eyeshadow.

A piece of jewelry hung from a chain around her neck— a triquetra pendant. I wore a similar charm but hid it beneath my faded yellow T-shirt. We were polar opposites, even in personality, but we got along well enough.

I rang up a half-caf Americano for Mrs. Richman, a middle-aged cat shifter. Trish made the drink and put it on the counter. And from our separate vantages, we both watched Mrs. Richman leave.

There was a note of apprehension in the air, waiting for

another customer to replace Mrs. Richman's car outside. When no one came, we sighed in unison.

"All right," Trish said. "Care to explain the disaster zone that is Orange Blossoms? I'm guessing I won't be getting fajitas anytime soon."

"They weren't the best fajitas." I poured myself a cup of coffee and stirred in a packet of sugar.

"Not the point. I saw your text. I read it. Several times, in fact. And yet, I still don't understand what happened last night."

I shrugged. "A ghoul attacked the restaurant. I, um, stopped it."

"Okay. Yeah, that's exactly what the text said. I need, like, every other detail."

I filled her in, just as I had Twinkie.

Trish's brow furrowed deeper and deeper. "Okay. So, I get what happened. My last question is why?"

"Why did I stop it?" I asked.

"No. Why did it attack the restaurant?"

I shrugged again. "Your guess is as good as mine."

"Not true."

"It was looking for a crowded place," Twinkie said. "They're drawn to crowds. It's how ghouls work."

"You have a lot of experience with ghouls?" Trish asked.

"None."

"And you?" Trish asked. "Why do you think it was there? Was it after you?"

"Maybe. Maybe not." I stared down at my Chuck Taylors. "Honestly, I was kind of hoping you had an idea or two."

"Oh," she scoffed. "I have several. Each as crazy as the next. I mean, when you think about it, there's been a steady build of crazy around you. I think you're cursed."

"Obviously." I had to agree.

"Have you talked to your Gran about this?"

I shook my head.

Her brow went smooth in surprise. "You haven't? Not at all?"

"I couldn't call her last night. She'd be in bed. And it's not like she uses text."

Trish pointed toward the back door. "Get out of this store. Get out now, Constance Campbell. We'll continue this conversation when you've talked to an expert."

"Hey! I talked to Twinkie. And to Brad."

"Experts have practical, not theoretical, knowledge."

"I heard that." Behind her familiar's voice, Twinkie's vessel— the mouse—squeaked.

"And do you disagree?" Trish called out.

"No." She squeaked again, more meekly than before.

Trish jabbed her finger forcefully at the door.

There was nothing I could do but follow it.

FOR THE SECOND time in a row, and maybe the second time ever, I had to use my key to get into Gran's house. I unlocked the door, felt her wards wash over me as I walked inside, and scoured the first floor for Gran.

I checked outside in the garden. No sign of her. And unlike when I'd bound Custos, her car was there in the garage—parked in its usual spot.

She was here somewhere—my gift told me that was true.

"Gran?" I called up the stairs.

Again, no answer.

She's probably taking a nap.

There was no familiar around to confirm or deny that thought.

Then I heard a loud *thump* from overhead. So, she was awake. Not for the first time, I wondered how I got stuck with the world's most frustrating grandmother.

"Gran, I know you're up there."

She didn't answer.

I was going up.

The stairs creaked under my feet. Otherwise, the house was quiet again.

But Gran wasn't in bed. She wasn't in the bath either—I knocked, then went inside. My old room was empty too.

I questioned my gift. She couldn't be home. Or so I thought. Until I heard another loud thump from somewhere above my head. And this time, I was on the second floor.

What the heck?

In the hallway, the attic door was closed. I tugged on the string anyway. I unfolded the ladder and went up the rickety, partially rotted steps.

"Up, girl. Get up here. And close it after you. You're letting the cold air out."

A sauna-like humidity hit my face like a wave. It clung to my body as I eased up into the stooped attic space. "What cold air?"

"Trust me. It's colder than what it was." She pointed a gnarled finger to the window unit at the end of the room. It shook and hissed, working overtime. "Cold air sinks. Now, close that door."

The attic was Gran's witching space. Even when I lived here, I'd hardly ever seen her use it. Especially not during the heat of the day. And this was the heat of an especially hot summer day.

Having watched *National Lampoon's Christmas Vacation*

too many times to count, I wrenched the ladder up with some trepidation. It sprang closed with a not-so-satisfying *slam* of wood against wood.

"You're sure this is a good idea?"

"It's a bit late to question it," Gran quipped. "To date, I've never gotten stuck. It's a simple enough spell to open it again."

"All right." I breathed a little easier—but not that easy because the air was so muggy and hot. "And you say this thing is working?" The closer I got to the window unit, the surer I was the racket it made was for show.

"If I say it is, then it must be."

Gran had jerry-rigged the air conditioner to what was supposed to be a vent—not an actual window.

It wasn't the only modification to the attic. Some were handy, some magical. The wooden planks she'd nailed to the beams made a mostly even attic floor. The lights, however, were artificial—just spheres of yellow hanging in the air. I'd asked about them once, and she told me she got tired of replacing bulbs.

I tried to tell her about fluorescents; it went over about as well as most of my suggestions did.

She'd made the attic a real workspace over the years. There was an old bookshelf with a few neat stacks of books. Between them, there were containers of dried herbs and glass jars filled with the pickled anatomy of lesser creatures. A small cauldron, no bigger than a five-gallon bucket, sat unused in the middle of the room.

Gran hunched over a sewing table. The sewing machine was stored in my old room. On this table, in its place, there was a spinning wheel straight out of *Sleeping Beauty*. Beside it, there were odds and ends—some dice, a seashell or two, and loose pieces of jewelry. Gran's ruby ring and a necklace, similar to the one we'd found on the ghoul.

What interested me most was the object Gran held in her knobby, arthritic fingers. It was a hand mirror.

"What is it?" She scowled.

"Mirror, mirror, in your hand. I thought we got rid of every mirror in the land?" It wasn't a very good rhyme, nor was it true. But we had gotten rid of every mirror in the house. Or so I thought.

She set it down, her lips pressed tightly together.

Looking at Gran was like looking in a funhouse mirror—one that adds a few lines around your face. We shared the same blue eyes. In poor lighting—like in a dim attic lit by magical balls—my dirty blonde hair could be mistaken for her gray with its auburn highlights. Except hers was a lot shorter and messier than mine.

"In the land?" Gran scoffed. "No. We did get rid of every mirror in the house. Every mirror except this one. I guarantee you haven't done the same at your new abode."

"You'd be right about that. I doubt Dave would approve."

"Why? Does he have one above the bed?"

"Gran!"

She cackled. "Learn to take a joke, Constance. Seriously, though. With your luck, you should consider removing those mirrors. You never can be too careful. Not with all the demons and spirits we've seen over the last year. And what's this I heard about a ghoul?"

"How did you hear about it?"

"I have my ways. And the Facebook."

"Okay. It's, uh, it's actually why I came over." I raced through an explanation. I wanted to get to the point—and out of the wretched heat of the attic.

Gran said nothing. She barely acknowledged I'd said

anything—let alone been talking for the past however many minutes.

"Well?" I nudged.

"Well, what?"

She knew why I was here. There was no beating around that bush. Maybe she was tired of it—tired of me coming to her with all my problems. Even if she was the cause of half of them.

Had she just told me about the magical mine, instead of shirking her responsibility as caretaker, it might still be intact.

And ghouls wouldn't be popping up to attack me.

I sighed. "Do you have anything to offer? Any insight?"

"None whatsoever."

"None?"

"I've never dealt with a ghoul before. Only heard about them this morning. Do you really think I've handled everything?"

I shrugged.

"Well, I haven't."

"Noted."

Gran picked up the mirror, angling it so I couldn't see the reflection.

It piqued my interest. "Hey—if I'm supposed to get rid of my mirrors, why do you have this one? Did you always have it up here?"

Gran nodded. "The charms on this room keep it safe. This is a one-way mirror."

"One-way?"

"You remember, mirrors can be like windows into other worlds?"

I nodded. I knew better than most. The demon Beruth had used the rearview mirror in my car to lock eyes with me.

This enabled her to slip into my subconscious and possess my mind. She caused a nasty wreck.

"There are a few things I need to check into."

I leaned over to get a peek, and she angled it away again. When I tried to follow it, I hit my head on the ceiling.

"Ouch."

"Serves you right." She pressed the mirror to her chest. "Come on. Let's get downstairs. It's stifling up here."

"Now you admit it." I rubbed my forehead.

Gran eased off her stool and limped to the ladder door. She pointed. "Down you go. Nice and slow."

The door didn't budge.

"What's up with that?"

"We are." She glared at me, then glowered at the door. "It always works. Why didn't it work?"

"Here. Let me try." I gathered my thoughts and put together a simple rhyme, calling to my magic. "Open up. What's the holdup?"

Nothing happened.

The bit of magical exertion caused my brow to sweat.

"You can't end a spell with a question," Gran huffed. "And it was you that brought this heat up." She waggled her finger at the window unit. "Don't withhold. Make it cold."

This time, the magic took. In a few short seconds, we went from furnace to freezer. The temperature plummeted.

"Seriously?" My teeth were chattering.

"Try pushing it open." Gran used a shaky arm to gesture toward the attic door.

I tried to force it open with a foot. The other stayed firmly rooted next to the sill. When that didn't work, I put my full weight on the door. It still wouldn't budge. Suddenly, I was feeling claustrophobic. My heart began to beat hard enough I could feel it in my chest.

"The magic must want us here," Gran said. "Best we figure out why."

"Maybe it just wants us to freeze to death in the middle of summer."

"Oh, I can fix that."

She couldn't though. The spell on the window unit continued to barrage us with ice cold air, even after I unplugged it.

I kicked at it. "Magic is so—"

"Finicky?" she offered.

"Unpredictable," I finished.

"That's not exactly true. Magic works when it wants to work. When it must work. If it wants us up here, it has a good reason."

"Maybe it wants you to tell me about ghouls," I offered.

"I already told you I don't know anything about them. It's not that. It's something else—something connected."

"Isn't everything connected in some way?"

"It is."

I kicked one last time at the door, then it hit me what it must be. We never spoke about the mine. Not directly.

"It's the mine," I said. "I need to tell more people about it."

"People?" She narrowed her eyes. "You mean the Faction."

"Should I tell them?"

She inclined her head. "Use your best judgment. They might be allies, but they have their own priorities. Are they going to help with your mother, finally?"

"I think so."

Gran brought the mirror up from her chest, checked it, and put it down on the sewing table.

"What are you checking on?"

"Right now?" she replied. "Nothing important."

"Okay... what were you checking on when I came up here?"

"Oh. That *is* important." She shivered slightly, either from the cold or the subject change. "I was checking in on the Mother."

"The Mother? As in, Mother Gaia? Mother Earth?"

"The very same."

"I didn't realize she was someone you could check in on."

"If you know where to look."

I sighed. "I hate when you're cryptic. Spill. Tell me what this is all about."

"It's complicated. I'm not sure I should."

Using my foot, I tapped on the door. "We're still trapped up here. I asked about the mine. You do your part."

"It's complicated," she said.

"With you, it always is." My mind wasn't racing, not as my body was busy fighting the cold. But it found its way onto a path. "Wait... did the Mother give you a gift? Something other than that extra year?"

Gran's smile wasn't pretty, but I had clearly struck a chord. "Not exactly," she said. "I think—I think she imparted some part of herself to me. It's in you as well. It's just a feeling I have."

"What's it feel like?"

"Like danger," she said.

"Like Mother Gaia's in danger?"

"Somehow, I think she is."

I reached into my own gift. And I could feel it too.

"You understand she is the binding?" Gran asked. "In some ways, Mother Gaia *is* the shadow realm. She connects our world to the others. Through her, all magic flows. Should something happen to her, well, I think you get it."

"But she's the Mother. She can't—"

"Few beings are all powerful, Constance. Even immortals. Especially immortals. Bullets may not graze their skin, but their lives are confined by the laws they're bound to uphold."

That was a profound statement. One I hadn't considered before. "Like familiars...They're bound by laws."

Weirdly, it was all starting to make a sort of sense. Gran's wariness of familiars—even her own.

"Where is Stevie right now?" I asked. "Where are the other cats?"

"At the groomer. They needed a bath. Stevie especially. He hates them"

"Wait." I gave in to a shiver, rubbing my bare arms for some heat. "You went to somewhere the other day, *and*—" I emphasized the word "—to the groomer today? Who are you, and what have you done with my grandmother?"

"I knew it was you who'd been in my garage," she said. "And I never said *I* went to the groomer's."

"Then who did?"

On cue, the door downstairs opened and shut. There was a shuffle of feet and a pitter patter of paws.

"Who's that?"

"That," Gran announced with a sly smile, "is my apprentice."

7

THE APPRENTICE

"You... you have an apprentice?"

Gran shrugged. "It used to be you."

The attic door eased open. I craned my head toward the opening.

Below us, Summer Shields, the pointy-faced channel seven reporter, lifted her chin. She stroked the cat in her arms like she was a James Bond villain.

Summer was the former cohost of a speculative supernatural podcast called *Creel Creek After Dark,* and that—among some *other* reasons—made her a former nemesis of mine. We hadn't exactly made nice, but we were no longer feuding.

Like many other Creel Creek residents, Summer was sensitive to magic. Like me, she never knew anything about it. Until she turned forty. And after an unpleasant encounter in the magical mine, she was now a full-blown witch—if a tad less powerful than the rest of us, but still a witch.

Beside her, at the base of the ladder, was Gran's familiar Stevie, looking regal with his graying mane washed and combed. He had the look of a Maine Coon, his face squashed and pensive.

"Nice to see you again, Constance," his deep throaty voice bellowed.

"Thanks," I said. "You too." I gave him and Summer a nice view of my rear end as I scaled the ladder down to the hallway.

"You get trapped up there again?" Summer asked Gran.

"Again?" I stumbled on the bottom step. "You mean this has happened before?"

"Every day this week," Summer replied.

"Gran!" I scolded. "Why in the world would you trap me up there?"

"Technically, you trapped yourself." Gran took the steps laboriously, one at a time. "It's part of an experiment I'm working on—using the scientific method on my magic."

"And how's that working out for you?"

She shrugged. "One day, those stairs will lower. I guarantee it."

I rolled my eyes so only Summer could see. "This is who's teaching you magic?"

She grinned. "Why don't we go to the kitchen? I can make us some tea. Or coffee."

"Tea," I said at the same time Gran chimed, "Coffee."

"Or both," Summer offered.

It was quiet downstairs except for the clock ticking. We were all at a loss for words. Until we weren't. We all started in at once, the words muddled together.

I cleared my throat. "What's this all about? You're teaching Summer? You're learning from Gran?"

Gran frowned. "I'm not trying to replace you, if that's what you think."

"It's not. It's *really* not. I'm more worried about her."

"Me?" Summer asked.

"Yes. You." With a head bob, I indicated Gran. "She can't just have you do things for her and call it an apprenticeship. I mean, it's what I did, but I'm her granddaughter. And I lived here rent free."

"It's a bit more than that," Summer said slowly, as if she were doing the math in her head.

Gran sipped a cup of coffee and stared blankly at the kitchen wallpaper.

"What are you getting out of it then?"

"She's teaching me magic."

"Right," I mocked. "I'm sure she is. Let's hear it. Let's hear what you've learned."

"I've, uh, well… I can shock things."

"If I recall, you could do that much a few months ago."

"I'm better at it now."

"What about potions?" I asked. "What about the Mother, do you know about her? Has Gran taught you about magic and need—how they go hand in hand?"

"I'm sitting right here," Gran said sourly. "You can't just talk around me like I'm not."

"I can. And we will. You should've told me you were teaching Summer magic—if you really even are."

"Why? Why should I have told you?"

"Because *I* was going to teach Summer magic."

"You were?" Summer scrunched her pointed nose.

"I was." I shrugged. "I was planning to… eventually."

"Could've fooled me." Summer's tone dripped with sarcasm. "You never answered my text from two weeks ago."

"I, uh, I meant to." It was the truth. I couldn't help I was a busy person.

"So—" Gran slurped some coffee "—what I'm hearing is, we made the right decision."

"Sure. Whatever you say. I'd still like to know what you've taught her—if anything."

"Focus," Gran answered. "I've taught her to focus. Something you could use as well."

"Cause you're the authority on that." My tone was similar to Summer's.

"You aren't getting my meaning." Gran set her coffee cup down. "You should focus, dear. Focus on yourself. You aren't a green witch any longer, but you aren't ripe enough to take on a student, either."

"I thought the best way to learn was to teach."

"Oppenheimer wasn't a witch," Gran replied. "Besides, you've got enough on your plate. Tell me what you found out about ghouls."

"I'd like to know too," Summer said. "Did you see what happened at Orange Blossoms?"

"I, uh, I did." I rubbed my temples. "So, she's how you knew about the ghoul?"

Gran shrugged.

"She really doesn't get out much," Summer said.

"Except for the other day," I put in. Gran was still being cagey about where she'd been.

"Is that when you went to the funeral?" Summer asked her.

"Might've been." Gran frowned. She didn't like anyone airing her business. Her secrets. Even if it wasn't much of one.

"Who died?" I asked.

"No one you know. I do have *other* friends. Or I did. Just be glad she isn't here right now. Knowing this one, she's off haunting someone."

"Really?" Summer looked skeptical.

I wasn't. I'd seen a few ghosts before, including my

father's. I doubted this person had the leftover business required to become a ghost.

"Maybe," Gran said. "Maybe not."

"Okay." I shook off her comment. "Well, where was Stevie then?"

"I was in the shadow realm," he said. "I, too, have other friends. And I'd prefer not to be brought into this."

"Into what?"

"This business," he boomed. "Any of it. Arguing with your grandmother. Training this one. I don't like any of it."

"About that." Summer looked to Gran. "What's on the docket today?"

Gran drained her coffee, got up, and shuffled toward the den. "I'm afraid the lessons are over for today."

Gran grabbed the remote from the arm of her chair and turned the television on with a pronounced gesture.

"Why?" Summer followed her. "I cleared my whole afternoon. My whole evening."

"I'm tired," Gran said.

Summer's pointed features fell flat. With her sad eyes, she looked like a dachshund.

Before I knew it, I was feeling sorry for her. Words tumbled out of my mouth. "That's all right, Summer. You can come with me. There are a few people I'd like you to meet."

"Seriously? Where?"

What did I mean? Why did I say that?

I struggled a moment and said, "The Creel Creek Mountain Lodge."

She winced. "You know, I'm not sure I'm allowed to go there anymore. Not after the bird incident. That was you, right?"

I made a similar face. "It was. But in fairness, it was a bad situation *you* put me in. I say let's chance it."

She shrugged and agreed to come along.

Gran just shook her head. "More of the blind leading the blind."

"Except," I said, "you're the one who needs glasses."

I was proud of my little comeback. But when I got to the door and twisted the handle, I remembered the pair of readers tucked away in my purse.

Getting old sucks.

8

IN WITCH WE DRINK

Two highways intersected in the middle of Creel Creek. From Gran's house, I took one to the other. Summer followed my Subaru Outback, Prongs, a little too closely in her little red coupe. Prior to this, I'd only ever seen her in a news van, chauffeured by her grizzly bear of a cameraman.

We took the highway to the outskirts of town. There wasn't much—a newer Walmart, the old high school, and farther down the road, the Creel Creek Mountain Lodge, a resort style hotel that catered to weddings mostly.

A golf course surrounded the property. The original hotel, with its grandiose lobby, was made of logs, with a green roof. The additional buildings—the conference center and facilities for the golf course—were stone. Overall, it looked like a giant mashup of Lincoln Logs and a peculiar set of Legos.

Summer pulled into the spot next to me. I hopped out and led the way. I had a general idea of where I might find who we were going to meet.

The outside bar was nestled in a courtyard, between the lobby, the conference building, and the clubhouse.

Being such a small town, the lodge hosted as many locals as out-of-towners. And it seemed the party had started early.

A waterfall burbled opposite the bar, doing its best to drown out a gaggle of women doing karaoke on a small stage. They had on matching name tags and were singing the 90s anthem "Wannabe" by the Spice Girls.

"It looks like their conference got over early," I said.

"Looks like it." Summer nudged me. "I call dibs on "Don't Stop Believin'" when they're done."

"All yours." I smiled, despite myself.

"Who are we looking for again?" Summer shielded her eyes, scouring for people she didn't know.

Slate was easy to spot. He towered over everyone. Behind him, Ivan blended in with the scenery—the tall plants and brick walls.

"Found them," I said.

At the same time, they found us.

"Constance!" Slate beamed. "And friend."

"Summer." She offered the tall black man her hand.

"Nice to meet you," he said. "I'm getting you a drink. And not just because it's happy hour and my next one's free. No. I'm getting you a drink because it looks like you need one."

"You read my mind." Summer scampered behind him toward the bar, asking, "You can't really do that, can you?"

Ivan chuckled and nudged a glass of wine my way. "I had a feeling you'd show up."

"A feeling, huh?"

"Drink your wine. I'll explain when the whole party is here."

I shrugged and took a sip. It was good. I knew this wine well. It was from our local winery, Armand Vineyards—owned by my friend Cyrus Tadros.

Slate and Summer returned a few minutes later, both carrying drinks in each hand. I gave Summer a hard look. "Don't worry," she said. "Guess who's impervious to poisons?"

"Hilda?" I questioned.

"A late birthday present." Summer frowned. "She could've just got me a card."

"That reminds me." Ivan produced a leatherbound book from his back pocket. "Inductions are in order."

"For who?" I had already seen that book of his—the register. It listed every member of the Faction. Those who had been—their names were crossed out—and those who were to come. My name had appeared on the list, but faintly, until I agreed to join, and then it darkened to black on the page. I saw it with my own eyes and saw my mother's name there, too.

It was crossed out but different than the others, like it was written in pencil—like someone could fill it out in pen and read it again.

Or like it could be erased entirely.

"Induction for our new member," Ivan said. "Miss Summer Shields."

"That's how you knew I was coming." It was a fact. My gift verified it. "Her name appeared in the book."

I had to wonder if it was my own doing. After all, I'd invited Summer along.

Ivan narrowed his eyes. "You don't seem surprised."

"Actually, I am a little," I said. "But Summer's been full of surprises today."

"If it helps, I don't get what you two are talking about." She took a sip of some fruity cocktail.

"Fair enough," Ivan said. "We should probably tell you about ourselves. What do you already know?"

"Constance told me y'all are part of some secret order. Kind of funny to meet up in a hotel bar, isn't it?"

Slate set down his beer and leaned across the table. "Aren't hotel bars where the best spies do their dirty work?"

"I wouldn't know." Summer pushed the book back to Ivan, then she leaned closer to Slate. "Why should I join your shadowy organization?"

Slate inclined his head. "Besides the fact that we have cookies?"

She smiled coyly. "Forget the cookies for now. You can circle back to that. Why should I join?"

"You should join because then we'd get to hang out. And I'm a whole lot of fun."

"It's true," Ivan said.

"Okay. I'm asking you, whatever your name is—"

"Ivan."

"Okay. I'm asking you, Ivan. Why should I join?"

"It's simple really," he said. "There's power and protection in numbers. You can learn a lot from us."

"I already have a teacher," Summer countered.

"I know it's strange," Ivan said. "But I can't really explain until you join. And I already know you're going to join. It's just a matter of when."

"And if I don't want to?"

"It won't matter." Ivan shrugged.

"What Ivan is trying to say," I interjected, "is your name is written in his little book. It's called the register. It's magic. It tells him the future, in a way."

"It doesn't look written in stone." Summer's eyebrows knitted. "What if I refuse?"

"Eventually, you cave—like Constance here did."

"That's a great way to put it." I took a sip of wine.

"It's true though," Ivan said.

Rather than argue, I downed the rest of my wine.

"Let me think about it." Summer's eyes went to the empty stage—the Spiceless Girls had moseyed to the bar. "I'll tell you what. Come sing with me, and I'll join."

I nearly choked on my wine. She had to be kidding.

"Just like that?" Ivan asked.

"There's only one way to find out." Summer waggled her eyebrows.

"Isn't it a little early for karaoke?"

"It's midnight somewhere." Summer stood up and began to bop around to the background music. "Come on, Ivan. Live a little."

He shrugged and accompanied her to the stage.

Slate laughed into his beer. We watched as Summer and Ivan sang a poor rendition of the Journey classic and karaoke staple, "Don't Stop Believin.'"

The bar barely acknowledged them with a golf clap.

I thought they were done, but Summer wasn't stopping there. She forced Ivan to pick out a song and sing it solo.

Turns out, he can actually sing when he isn't forced into falsetto.

The crowd cheered as Summer encouraged him to sing another—there was currently no line for the microphone.

Ivan belted his way through "Pour Some Sugar on Me" and "Bittersweet Symphony." Before Ivan could get off the stage, Summer roped him into another duet.

While they were gone, Slate pulled me into a discussion.

"You know," he said. "It's rare to see that guy loosen up like this."

"I guess Summer has that effect on him."

"No. I don't actually think it's her." Slate's gaze fell on me. "It's you. When he's here, he has cover. He doesn't bear sole responsibility for protecting the paranormal world."

"That doesn't make sense though," I pointed out. "He always has the Faction backing him."

Slate shrugged. "I think it's hard for Ivan to differentiate between himself and the Faction. To him, they're one and the same. If we fail, he fails. To him, we're all just extensions of himself. Everyone, that is, except you."

"How do you feel about that?"

"I'm telling you how I feel about it," Slate said, not unkindly. "I don't like it. And it's not that I don't think Ivan is cut out for it. He is—he's our leader. I just don't think he should bear such a burden. Not alone. There has to be a dispersion of power."

"And that falls on me?"

"Not entirely." He shook his head. "But your abilities help. We were all surprised you took out that ghoul by yourself."

I shrugged. "It was pretty easy to beat."

Slate shook his head, his lips hovering over his beer. "You, my friend, got lucky."

Part of me wanted to protest—to tell him he was wrong, but I knew he was right. Still, I didn't think it was that big a deal either way.

"Okay... That's true. I did get a little lucky. And I understand why we don't want ghouls raging in the streets. But I don't see why facing a couple of ghouls, if that's what we have to do, is such a big deal."

"You don't see the big deal?" Slate was taken aback, his mouth agape.

"Now I know how to fight them. You just think happy or sad thoughts and hit it kinda hard."

"And?"

"And then, it goes…" I made an explosion with my hands.

"You really don't know, do you?" He sipped his beer, snickering to himself. "I hate to say Ivan's confidence in you is misplaced but…"

"But what?"

He set his beer down and stooped level to me. He was a big guy.

"Every ghoul is different," he said. "You, or maybe your familiar, guessed right."

I wasn't tracking.

He made a face as if he could tell. "All ghouls have a sort of kryptonite—a certain emotion they can't handle. Emotions, to ghouls, they're like a scent. It's how they locate their prey. Fear is like the best smell. It's like grilling a steak or walking into an ice cream factory."

"If it's like a scent, why would an emotion be able to destroy them?"

"Fair enough. It wasn't my best analogy. Let's try something else. Your car. It runs on gas, right? But it also needs oil. No. That doesn't work either."

In the middle of his explanation, Ivan and Summer returned. They were quiet, half watching the earlier trio, now returning to the karaoke stage. Surely, they were going to *spice up our lives* by performing a Spice Girls encore.

"Okay, bottom line," Slate continued, "ghouls are simple creatures. What you saw was that spirit wrapped in layers of flesh, blood, and other gunk—whatever it could find, really. And it was held together by some element of magic.

"They have few needs and fewer senses. You didn't actually kill that ghoul. Ghouls are spirits of the shadow realm. Like all spirits of the shadow realm, they can only be killed in the shadow realm."

"Then what the heck happened to it?" I asked.

"You put a bad taste in its mouth. Or to go back to my previous analogy, a bad smell in its nose, causing it to come apart. If that doesn't make any sense, talk to me again when I haven't had so many of these." He held up his empty beer.

"That actually made plenty of sense," I said.

"Not to me." Summer waved.

"I can explain once you officially join," Ivan told her.

"Fine, I join. Nice singing, by the way."

His face, including his ears, went red. "Thanks."

I stared at the redhead. "You're really going to join, just like that?"

She shrugged. "I don't see any way around it. Plus, I'm guessing there are more perks. I've had gym memberships like this before. You know, the ones with the pizza."

"Free pizza." Slate went to clink glasses and realized his was empty. "I'm in need of another round."

"As am I," Ivan said, then tipped his head toward me. "Are you down for another?"

"I don't know. I have to text Dave and tell him I'll be home late."

"Do it,' Summer encouraged.

I rolled my eyes and pulled out my phone. While I did that, Ivan brandished his book and pushed it back Summer's way.

She opened the register and flipped a few pages. "That looks familiar."

"What does?"

"The handwriting." I'd forgotten how eerie it was to see my own name filled out in my own handwriting—knowing I had nothing to do with the writing.

Slate returned, drinks in hand. "You know what else is familiar? Your voice."

Ivan chuckled. "That's because we listened to it most of the way from San Diego. She's on the *Creel Creek After Dark* podcast."

"No. I *was* on the podcast," Summer corrected.

"Not anymore?"

She shook her head. "Not for a while now. Besides, the way Jade's handling things, it's only a matter of time before there is no podcast. She's losing subscribers in droves."

"That's too bad," Ivan said.

"You really think so? I thought you'd hate the podcast. I mean, no offense, but we always tried to expose your kind." She sighed. "I'd be lying if I said my heart wasn't still in it a bit. Especially now. Knowing what I know. Jade was right. Magic exists."

Ivan nodded. "I'm actually of the opinion the podcast does some good for our community. Most of its followers are paranormals in hiding."

Slate seemed to agree. "I wish we could help."

Ivan considered. "Maybe we can."

"*We* can?" Summer looked skeptical. "As in all of us?"

Ivan grinned into his drink. "I have a few ideas."

9

CREEL CREEK AFTER DARK
EPISODE 107

It's getting late.
Very late.
The creeping dread of tomorrow haunts your dreams.
It's dark out. Are you afraid?
Welcome to Creel Creek After Dark.

I'm your host Ivana Steak. Welcome to yet another episode of *Creel Creek After Dark*.

Today is the day. We're going live. Correction. I'm going live.

I'll be answering your questions in the live chat, taking your calls, and answering any new emails that have come our—my way.

Why do I still say we all the time?

Never mind.

Here's our first email.

Hi... My name is Jim Carpenter. Long time listener. I was just wondering when Athena was going to be back on the air? The show's been kind of lacking with only a single host. I hope she'll be back soon. Why don't you ever talk about her? Did something happen?

Sure. I've been mum on this topic for a while. I figured you'd get the hint. Athena's status is the same. She took up with the witches. There are currently no plans for her to come back on the air.

Next email.

Hello. My name is Hank Heller. I've lived in Creel Creek all my life, and it wasn't until listening to this show that my eyes were opened.

You're right. This town isn't what people think it is. I really enjoyed the episodes about the winery and that ghost writer.

I do have a question though. Where's Athena been? I haven't heard her voice in a while...

Ugh!

Let me quickly remind everyone, not only can you find us on your favorite podcast platforms, but you can now find the show on ParaTube—where I'm live right now.

Our toll-free number is listed on the bottom of the screen. If you'd like to call and ask a question, please do so now.

Also, if you happen to have footage of any supernatural event—say whatever *really* happened at Orange Blossoms the other night—we'd love for you to send it our way.

Sorry, again, I'd love for you to send it *my* way.

Let me just check the chat real quick.

Yeah. Real funny. I'm blocking you.

And you.

Okay. Never mind. No chat. Let's take a caller.

Ivana: Hello, caller one, you're on the air...

Caller One: Hi, uh—

Ivana: Caller one, you need to turn your speakers down. I'm getting a lot of feedback.

Caller One: Is this better? Can you hear me?

Ivana: Much... much better. Yes. I can hear you. How are you today, Bobo?

Caller One: Uh, well, I'm all right. It's been dead quiet around here until the other day. Anyway, I'm with those emails. I've been wondering about Athena...

Ivana: Like I already said—and for the millionth time—there are no plans for Athena to come back to the show. And Bobo, please refrain from calling my private number. I needed pest control, not a new friend.

Caller One: Those can go hand in hand.

Ivana: Umm. Let's try caller number two. Hello, caller two, are you there?

Caller Two: I'm here, Ivana. Thanks for taking my call. As they say, long time listener, first time caller. I'm a big fan of yours.

Ivana: Do you happen to have a question for me? One that isn't about Athena Hunter?

Caller Two: I believe I do.

Ivana: You do?

Caller Two: I think so.

Ivana: Well, isn't that great? I was about to give up.

Caller Two: Don't give up on us yet, Ivana. We might surprise you.

Ivana: I'm sure you might, caller two. And your question is?

Caller Two: It's a simple question. I was actually wondering if I could show you some magic?

10

IN WITCH I'M HUNGOVER

"It looks like you had an eventful night." While Dave's voice was better than any alarm clock, it was still an unwelcome wake-up.

My head was pounding. My throat was dry. And my eyes weren't up to the task of opening.

I blinked against the surprising amount of light in the room.

"Wha—what time is it?" I sounded far too much like the singer of the Crash Test Dummies.

"Well, technically, it's still morning," Dave said in answer. "But only just."

I reached for the glass of water beside the bed. I didn't remember putting it there. Then again, I didn't remember a lot about the previous evening.

How many songs had I sung?

How many drinks had I drunk?

The scratchiness of my throat answered a lot to both questions.

"Mmm Mmm Mmm Mmm." I cleared my throat.

Did I sing that too?

I rolled over to find Dave, fully clothed atop the covers. He leaned against the headboard balancing a tablet on his midsection. He was reading.

"That's not an exact time," I said.

"It's almost noon.

"So, technically, it's morning. At least for a few more minutes."

I struggled, my brain feeling as thick and slow moving as my saliva. If it was truly that late, why were we still in bed? And why wasn't I at work?

Then I remembered it was Sunday. Our lazy day. The bookstore was closed. We had the whole day to do whatever we wanted.

Make that half a day. I'd promised to take the girls shopping.

"Where are the girls?"

"Imogene took them to the pool after breakfast."

"I missed breakfast." My stomach grumbled.

"You're pretty close to missing lunch too," he said.

"What was it?" I asked. Sunday breakfast was the best breakfast.

"Cinnamon rolls and bacon. I'll let you guess how much there is left."

I knew the answer. The sunlight in the room was making a lot more sense. "Why'd you let me sleep in so long?"

"Unlike you," he said, "I'm not well-versed in waking the dead."

I rolled my eyes and twisted out of the comforter, heading for the bathroom. I had to make room if I wanted to down the water beside the bed, which I very much did. My throat felt like sandpaper.

Seriously, how many songs did I sing?

I disappeared into the bathroom. There, I tried to piece

together my memories but only found flashes—me on stage with Ivan and Slate. And Summer and I sang too.

Oh, and we joined the Spiceless Girls for a number. If I had to guess, I was Witchy Spice.

"You're right," I said, returning to the comfort of the bed. "It was an eventful night. I wish I remembered more of it."

"Yeah—you haven't really let loose like that since we met. I was a little surprised by it."

"In what way?" I asked.

"In many ways," he answered. "But if pressed into what surprised me most, well, that honor would go to *how* you got home."

"I didn't call you?"

He shook his head. "Summer Shields dropped you off."

My dry mouth fell open. "I don't even remember that."

"That's probably for the best." He chuckled.

"Why? Did I say something?"

"Uh. Let's see. When I helped you out of the car, you told her you loved her and that you were going to make sure your Gran treated her right. I'm not sure I should say the rest. In fact, let's not dwell on it. You were in pretty bad shape."

"I used to be able to hold my liquor." I huffed. "Sorry. I don't know what got into me last night."

I did know I was paying for it though. My head throbbed.

Dave handed me a bottle of pain relievers and indicated the water. "You needed it. Everyone deserves a break every now and again."

His words reminded me of what Slate had said about Ivan. How Ivan had so much on his shoulders. And here, in Creel Creek, he could relax a little.

Or could he?

Could I?

Could anyone?

Ivan wasn't the only person I knew who put so much on their shoulders. As sheriff, Dave held the weight of the whole town. That meant not only crime but anything out of the ordinary.

Anything supernatural.

I gave him a hard look. "If that's true, then when are you going to take a vacation?"

"Not anytime soon." He chuckled again. "I, too, am recovering from an eventful day."

"Yeah?" I took the medicine and gave him my full attention.

"First, I tracked down the necklace. Or I think I did. There were plenty of old cases to sort through, but I think I found the right one. It was likely stolen from Rosemary's Antiques."

"Is that the barn-looking place out toward the vineyard? I always wanted to check it out."

"What's stopped you?"

I shrugged a shoulder. "Trish told me the prices were exorbitant."

"I've heard that too. But to be fair, I wouldn't know what to pay for a restored rocking chair made in the Great Depression."

"Would you mind if I delivered the necklace?"

"Would I mind?" He scoffed. "That'd be great. There's just one problem. Rosemary Owens, the owner of the place, she died last week."

I sat up, making my head spin.

He put up his hands. "It's nothing sinister. The old broad was ninety-six. She passed the store down to her daughter Ellen. I only know her by reputation. I've heard she's kind of a trip. Anyway, that wasn't really the eventful part."

"No? Then what was?" I massaged my temples.

"We must've got fifty, maybe sixty calls—all about the happenings at Orange Blossoms. People in the know. People out of the know. It didn't matter. They wanted to know what I'm going to do to stop something like that ever happening again."

"That's not good," I said.

"The mayor thinks we should hold some sort of meeting—a town hall. People are afraid this isn't an isolated incident."

"It's not," I said, wishing I could disappear as Dave's eyes became narrow slits.

"Did you say it's not?"

I flinched and nodded.

"Meaning what?"

"Meaning stuff like this has been happening across the country."

"The Faction," he said under his breath. "Do they know why it's happening? Do they have a solution? Anything I should know about?"

"I think we're all playing catch up. You know they want to stop things like this from happening. It's kind of what they do."

"That's good." Dave went quiet for a second. He grimaced, looking as if he was going to tell me something, but shook his head. "Hey," he said, "how about I let you rest a little while longer while I scrounge up lunch? I might even know where a cinnamon roll was hidden."

"You do?"

"Maybe." He smiled. "That's if I don't eat it first."

"You wouldn't."

His smile got broader, and he pecked my forehead.

I sank into my pillow and closed my eyes. I didn't sleep, though. Instead, I got lost in my own thoughts.

In addition to ghouls, there was a demon to contend with. There were the secrets of the mine. And there was my mother. All were subjects I'd yet to fully divulge to Dave.

This is what great couples do, I thought.

They start conversations and pick them up when it's convenient. Or I thought that's what they might do. Maybe not all great couples. Maybe just some great couples. But what I realized—what I'd been realizing—was we were a great couple.

For a while, there'd been some thoughts nagging in the back of my head. The notion that we were rushing into things.

And maybe we were at first.

Our relationship started on the heels of the emotional train wreck that was my last marriage. Dating Dave and moving in together had gone quite fast.

A lot had happened since then.

A lot of good things. Some bad.

The timing, for all of it, had been perfect.

We weren't rushing now. We had slowed down. Or maybe we just found the perfect gear.

You just know when you find the right person; they don't take away from you, they add. And Dave, well, he multiplied.

"I mean it." He was back in the doorway, holding a plate of food—cinnamon roll and all.

"You mean what?" Maybe I wasn't as good at continuing our conversations as I'd imagined being.

"I mean it's good they're so invested—the Faction, that is.

I could use some help. Especially if something like this should happen again."

"Definitely," I agreed.

He handed me the plate. "Can I ask you something though? Promise not to get mad?"

I realized this was the continuation from when he'd grimaced—when he'd held something back. Dave was much better at this than me.

"Promise." I didn't know if it was possible to be mad at Dave—not while he was gifting me a cinnamon roll.

"If you don't mind," he said, "I'd like to talk to Ivan myself. It'd help if I got a clearer picture of what's been going on outside of Creel Creek. Not that hearing it secondhand isn't great but—"

"Dave," I said. "I get it. You want to be included."

11

BEWITCHED BOOKS

Ask anyone what the worst day of the week is, and it's guaranteed six out of seven will tell you Monday.

That jaded person who claims it's Wednesday is a bridge troll and cannot be trusted.

Mondays are the worst.

Bewitched Books used to close on Monday. When I got the espresso machine, that changed, and so did the hours—Mondays are prime coffee days as everyone needs that extra pick-me-up to charge up for the week ahead.

It was my own fault really.

What wasn't my fault—and what I failed to comprehend—was why Trish chose this godforsaken day of the week as the one to come in early.

On Mondays, the Trish-isms were most pronounced.

For the first hour, I steered clear of her, not even talking. I just acknowledged her grunts and eye rolls with nods and trepidatious smiles.

We made it through the first few customers without incident. Then I found a familiar raven perched at the window.

"Is that who I think it is?" Trish asked.

Vertigo was Ivan's familiar. He liked to roam ahead and scout things out.

"I, uh, didn't mention the Faction is in town?"

"It must've slipped your memory."

Ivan rolled in a few minutes later. He was alone this time. Dressed as always in shades of gray, still opting for pants and long sleeves despite the heat of summer.

There was no love lost between Trish and Ivan. She clucked her tongue at him but held her words as a customer came rushing in behind him.

The woman was in such a hurry, she hadn't noticed the raven she'd passed, still perched in the window with her wings outstretched.

Ivan pretended to peruse the bookshelves as I took the woman's order.

Trish gave the wizard a side eye, making the drink. She set it on the counter and shot the woman a brief smile.

That was the most hospitality anyone got from Trish.

It was short-lived though. The woman scooted out the door, then made a mad dash for her car when Vertigo swooped over her head.

"Thanks for that," Trish snarled.

"She has a mind of her own." Ivan winced a little. "Like any pet, she just wants to be acknowledged... and fed."

"Speaking of fed, do I have you to blame for that mess at Orange Blossoms? That ghoul or whatever."

Ivan held his hands up placatingly. "I got here the next morning."

"That's not exactly a no." Trish's green eyes narrowed. "You had a reason to be here. I'm guessing it had something to do with what happened."

He bobbed his head from side to side. "We thought Creel Creek was a likely target."

"And you were right," I said.

"Why here though?" Trish asked.

Ivan paced the length of a bookshelf, running his hand across the faded leather spines. "This place has more shadow realm openings than anywhere else. There's a single opening in all of New York State. Two in D.C. Another five across the whole United States, until you hit California where there's five or six. There's three between L.A. and San Diego. That's it. The whole country has fourteen, and Creel Creek has what, four?"

I counted on my fingers. He was right. "But that's counting the one at the vineyard. Technically, that's out of town."

"Technically, that's three too many," Ivan countered.

Trish's thin eyebrows furrowed. "What's that supposed to mean? It's not like we can do anything about those portals."

"Maybe we can." Ivan shrugged. "Maybe we can't. For now, we've got members posted at each one with a trace and an alarm spell to let us know if and when something goes in, or especially if something comes out."

"You can do that?" Trish asked.

"We can." Ivan nodded, but his eyes were scanning the shelves.

This was new information to me. In my mind, the portals were like invisible black holes. "Seriously? You can do this? Does it take a lot of magic?"

"It does. It's necessary for now. These measures are precautionary. We want to prevent future incidents."

"But aren't you kind of missing the bigger picture?" Trish asked him.

Ivan looked over to her, skepticism written across his face. "And that is?"

"Ghouls can't think for themselves. If they're getting out of the shadow realm, someone is letting them out. Someone is calling them."

"That's what the trace spells are for," Ivan said. "Not to trace where the ghouls go—we should do that as well—but they're to trace the summoning."

"Well then," Trish was momentarily taken aback, "by all means, continue."

I scowled at her. "I thought you said you didn't know anything about ghouls."

"No. I said to talk to your grandmother. Something I have to say to you a lot. I know she's arrogant, manipulative, and a tad mean, but your grandmother knows her stuff."

"Gran doesn't know about ghouls, though."

"So she tells you," Trish said. "She probably has other fish to fry. You know your Gran, always trying to save the world from her armchair."

"Actually, you might be on to something there." I wasn't going to mention Gran's trepidations about the Mother. Not with Ivan around. It was a slippery slope to other topics I wasn't ready to bring up.

Ivan perked up. "Is it other or bigger fish?" he asked. "Either way, it sounds like we might have some similar interests. I should get your grandmother's number."

"That just sounds weird," Trish said. "And speaking of idioms, I have a bone to pick with you. Was that your voice I heard on *Creel Creek After Dark* the other night?"

"Maybe. Why do you ask?"

"I assume you have a plan. Some sort of endgame?"

"Perhaps."

"Are you being cagey because you think I'll think your plan is dumb or because it's actually dumb?"

"A little bit of both." He looked sheepish. "Anyway, why do you listen to the podcast? I thought you hated the host. What's her real name again? Jade?"

"I like keeping tabs on the people I hold grudges against." She batted the purple streak of hair out of her eyes.

Ivan stifled a laugh and went back to studying the bookshelves. "My cousin's an Aries too."

Trish rolled her eyes. "So, these spells you're putting on the portals—how many are active now?"

"We actually haven't set them up yet."

"Why not?" I asked.

"It's a little complicated. It's why I'm here. It works best if we have at least one person per portal."

"And you need me to take one."

Ivan nodded. "The one near your house—near Dave's house. And Trish, if you're up for it, the portal up the road here, by that park, that could be yours."

"I'm not joining the Faction," she said, a tad unkindly. In fairness, it was early on a Monday morning.

"I'm not asking you to join," Ivan said. "I'm asking if you'll help protect Creel Creek."

She scowled as she thought it over. "I guess... if only to make sure my other favorite restaurants don't get demolished."

"Great! Was that so hard?" Ivan beamed at her from the row of spell books in the back corner of the shop.

She rolled her eyes again and tucked the purple streak behind an ear.

"The alarm spell is Slate's specialty. He can teach you. I'll cover the trace. It's a lot like a summoning spell, which I hear you're pretty good at."

"Don't try to flatter me," Trish said.

"It really will get you nowhere," I added.

Ivan smiled again. He put a finger on a faded tome. "These are new, aren't they? I mean new to the shop, not *new* new."

"They are."

"When did they come in?"

"A few months ago, I guess. Our librarian brought them in." Trish said the word librarian like it was cursed.

It was my turn to roll my eyes. "That's because you never went back to the library to get them. She told you they were there."

"That lady gives me the creeps." Trish shuddered.

"Does she?" Ivan tipped a book out of its place. "I might have to meet this woman. Anyone who gives Trish the creeps is worth keeping an eye on."

"You really have a thing for octogenarians, huh?"

Ivan ignored her.

"She's like a hundred and ten," Trish continued. "And no matter how frail she looks, she's as strong as an ox."

"Part Fae in all likelihood," Ivan said.

"Maybe," I agreed.

"But you'll have to catch her tomorrow," Trish said. "The library's closed on Mondays." I sensed an air of envy in her tone.

"No matter. My schedule is jam-packed today as it is." He slid another few books off the shelf. "Did either of you take stock of these?"

Trish leaned over the coffee counter. "I looked them over. Why?"

"A hunch." Ivan spilled the books beside the register.

Trish came over and joined us. She flipped through the

first book and, not so carefully, shoved another in my direction.

I opened it and immediately closed it again, seeing a name etched on the first page. "Trish!"

"What?" She looked up, half startled. "Was there a spider in there? You know I hate spiders."

"What kind of witch hates spiders?" Ivan asked.

"The kind that doesn't mind hexing you. Say spider again."

Mondays.

The wizard opened then closed his mouth, thinking better of whatever comeback he had in mind.

I opened the book again and pressed my finger to the black ink on the page.

She looked down. "Oh!"

"What is it?" Ivan asked. "I feel like I'm missing something. Who is Nell Baker?"

"It's the book," Trish whispered.

"Y'all are toying with me now." He looked side to side. "What book? What is this exactly?"

"It's Nell Baker's spell book. Her grimoire. See? That's her name right there."

"I got that much. I'm still not following."

"A spell from this book was used to trap Brad in a sort of prison in the shadow realm."

"A prison? By who? This Nell lady?"

"No." I shook my head. "She died. A warlock did it. He died too. But more importantly, he had help."

"From?" Ivan arched an eyebrow.

"The entity in my mother's body. I think."

"Oh..." Ivan nodded solemnly. "This actually explains a lot—why you were so antsy around me when we first met, calling me a warlock and all that. I'm still a little offended, by the way."

"Sorry."

"Water under the bridge," he said. "I'd still like to know about the prison."

"For another time." I flipped through a few pages.

"This could be useful." He read over my shoulder. "Trapping a familiar is something we might need to do in the near future, right?"

"Right. Maybe. In theory." It still felt off when I tried to look for my mother's familiar. And no spell ever worked—no summoning spell, no tracking spell, nothing we tried. It was like he was off the map or something.

"All right, well, I think that'll do it." Ivan took an old potion book from the top of the stack. "I'll take this one." He pushed another in my direction. "And I have a feeling this is for you."

"Yeah, just take what you want," Trish quipped. "Not like I'm trying to run a business or anything."

"It looks more like a coffee business." We followed his gaze to a Suburban parking out front. "And it suits you."

Trish glowered at him.

Ivan winked. He headed for the door, turned, and said to me, "Secrets don't make friends, Constance. Take a look at that book. Hey, that rhymed! Anyway, I think it could be useful."

With that, he left.

Trish drummed her fingers on the counter, waiting for him to get out of sight. "What was that all about?"

"He knows I'm keeping a secret." I checked that Vertigo had gone too and mouthed, "About the mine. And the demon…"

"Ah. You don't want to tell him?"

"I do. It's just timing."

Trish nodded. She reached for the book Ivan had handed me. It looked just like all the others, if slightly thinner. The spine was a little less worn and the cover less faded.

When Trish tried to open it, the pages stuck together like glue. "What the junk?"

"What is it?" I held out my hand. "Let me see."

The book practically willed itself into my grasp, flying from her fingertips. It opened for me without issue.

"It's one of *those* books," she said slowly.

"Looks like it."

The book had the Faction written all over it, just not in any literal way. Inside, it looked like any other spell book. Or it did at first glance. I flipped through pages without really reading them.

There were no spells or potions. It was wall to wall text. All of which was handwritten and most of it in cursive. Each time I flipped a page, the pen changed, either to a different color or a different style of writing. I never seemed to hit a page twice. Either that or I was flipping through too fast to notice.

It reminded me of a family grimoire. But unlike Nell's, or even the grimoire Gran had handed down to me, there were no blank pages at the end.

I closed the book as the woman in the Suburban and her two children opened the door. Reading would have to wait.

"You know," Trish scooted toward the coffee counter, her eyes locked on the strange book, "I'm thinking maybe Ivan brought that book in here. I don't recognize it."

"You know," I said. "I bet you're right."

12

A BEWITCHED BOOK

Dave knew the Bewitched Books schedule almost as well as I did. Most days, he timed his arrival to beat the morning rush.

Today, he'd missed his usual appointment. His cup had stayed on the counter for a while before I poured it out in the sink.

He'd said he was busy with all the ghoul business. But too busy for coffee? That's not a thing.

It was nearing the lunch hour when his sheriff's department SUV finally pulled into the angled parking at the front of the store. His timing was impeccable. Trish had run off to find us something to eat, difficult now that Orange Blossoms was closed indefinitely.

I poured his coffee the way he likes it, yanked open a marker, and scrawled the word TARDY in bold letters on the side of the cup.

The handsome sheriff in his khaki uniform balked at it. "Does this mean I'm getting a demerit?"

"It's a warning," I said. "You could've called or texted. I had your coffee ready for you."

"I thought you'd be busy. Plus, I got distracted. Ivan stopped by earlier, almost as soon as I texted him."

"I guess he was making the rounds. He stopped in here too. How'd yours go?"

"It was a good talk," Dave said. "We agreed on a few things. Compromised on some others. I really want us to work together on this craziness. Put forth a solid front. Of course, you know this. But I wanted to articulate it to him in terms he could understand. It's one thing to go all supernatural vigilante across the rest of the country. Here, things are different. There's a chaotic order to it all, from the mayor and the folks at the league den on down."

"I'm sure Ivan understands."

"He does." Dave nodded. "And I understand a bit more about your organization."

"Probably more than I do at this point."

"Doubtful," he said. "But I believe the Faction could do a lot of good around here. And the way Ivan tells it, if things keep going the way they are elsewhere, I might have to deputize a few people."

"I can't tell if you're joking," I said.

"I'm not joking, Constance. We're already short-staffed. It's been months now, and I can't fill Willow's position—at least not with anyone who has a worthwhile set of skills."

"I don't think you'll find many people around here that see into the future."

He took a sip of his coffee. "Hell, I'm talking about basic skills. Verbal communication. Marksmanship. The ability to operate a motor vehicle. Yes, we had an applicant with a suspended license."

"When should I report for duty?"

He grinned. "Honestly, you're at the top of my list. Next

is that Slate guy—I just met him. Big dude. He'd be good in a fight against one of those ghoul things."

"Let's hope we don't have to deal with another one."

"That's the dream," Dave said. "Mostly, I'm worried about the next few days. And I'm really hoping this weekend is quiet."

"Why's that?" I wondered why this weekend was so important. It wasn't like he had to release a demon into the world.

"You don't remember?" He looked out the window as if the Moon were as high in the sky as the Sun. "It's my time of the month."

"Right...that."

Lately, I'd been so in my own head, so invested in everything else, I'd forgotten to keep track.

It wasn't as if watching the phases of the Moon was ever a pastime of mine. Not until I met Dave. The full Moon meant he, and a handful of others, shifted into their wolf forms. For two, maybe three nights—depending on light levels and various other factors—the girls and I would be alone at the house.

Unlike when he used the totem, Dave's moonlight shift came with consequences. He wasn't totally a monster, but he wasn't totally himself either. He didn't think before giving in to his urges.

Granted, it meant he could probably take out a ghoul. But who knew what *other* damage he might cause?

Reading the trepidation written across my face, Dave frowned. "If it's a problem," he said, "we can hire someone. I know a few shifters who are home for summer break."

"It's fine," I lied. His absence meant more work for me. And there were those other things we'd yet to discuss.

Demons. My mother and her familiar. And now, this book Ivan left for me.

I patted its cover. I hadn't gotten a chance to give it a real look. "You know what," I said. "Maybe it's a good thing you'll be gone for a couple nights."

"Yeah?" Dave sounded surprised.

"It'll give me some reading time. Ivan left me this book."

"Can I see?" Dave asked.

I handed it to him, completely forgetting the trouble Trish had trying to open it.

The same thing happened to Dave. He tried to pry it open but couldn't.

"Is this a prank book?" He grunted. "Is it glued shut? I don't want to rip it."

"I doubt you could." I gestured for it back, and again, it shot into my fingertips.

Dave's eyes went wide.

At my gentle touch, the book opened right up. "I think it's under a Faction spell—kind of like Ivan's book, the register."

"Weird."

I showed him a page and let him read over my shoulder. "What do you think?"

He shrugged. "I see words."

"Is that it?"

He hesitated. He bent down, squinting at the paper. A look of pure bewilderment crossed his face. "And I can't seem to read them. Well, I can read them individually, but they don't seem to stick in my head."

"That's weird." I read the first few lines on the page. "I can read them just fine. What if I read a sentence to you?"

"Go for it."

I read out loud something at random. "Did that stick?"

He shook his head. "In one ear, out the other. It's a lot like when I tell the girls to do their chores."

"Magic is weird," I said. "I'm going to have to test this out on Trish."

"She's going to *love* that." Dave pointed as if a thought had occurred to him. He dug in his pocket and pulled out a brown bag. "Here's that other magical artifact."

Dave shook the bag and emptied its contents. The necklace with its stone pendant slid out and landed beside the book. In the dim store, the stone was very dull. No shimmer at all.

It looked worthless. It would be, if there weren't that hint of magic in it. I wondered how much magic it once held. How much had the ghoul used to create its slimy body?

"Feel free to drop it off anytime between nine and three," Dave said. "Those are the antique store hours. That was a direct quote, by the way. When I talked to her earlier, she sounded a lot like she expected me to bring it by today."

"This is that Ellen lady? You said she was eccentric."

"I didn't say eccentric. I heard she was a character. And let's just say, the phone call did nothing to dispel the earlier assessment."

"Okay." I picked up the necklace. "I'm guessing you told her you were busy?"

"No. I told her you were going to deliver it. Remember? You offered?"

"I remember," I muttered.

"Can you do it?" he asked.

The back door of the shop opened and slammed. That would be Trish with lunch.

"I'll get it done," I told Dave and kissed him goodbye.

On top of everything else—on top of it being a Monday—I got to tell Trish I was leaving early.

She did not take it well.

13

MAGIC LOST, MAGIC FOUND

Over the course of the last year, I'd learned not to go alone basically anywhere in Creel Creek. It was better to have backup. There was no telling if I was conversing with a murderer, a supernatural hunter —a slayer of paranormals like me and everyone else—or knowing my luck, she'd be a sweet older lady possessed by a murderous demon.

Although the sunglasses would tip me off this time.

Worst case scenario, I'd find another dead body. There hadn't been any of those lately. It almost made Creel Creek feel like a normal town.

And normally, in situations like this, I'd lean on Trish. She was quick on her feet and a great conversationalist. This, despite her consummate crabby demeanor—and it being Monday.

But she'd refused to close early.

So, instead of Trish riding shotgun beside me in Prongs, and because I wasn't ready to speak to Ivan again, Summer Shields was there instead.

I know. I know.

I only had myself to blame. She was the first contact that came up on my phone's recent call list.

She smiled at me nervously from the passenger seat.

"Sorry if I don't remember anything I said the other night."

"Oh, I don't either," she said.

"Liar. I had that same alcohol immunity last year. And I know you don't have a goldfish memory like me. You and Trish remember everything."

"Oh, I know. She's hated me since high school. How is Miss Cold Topic? How much does she hate me being a witch?"

"Miss Cold Topic?" I questioned.

"You know. She gets all her clothes at Hot Topic. At least, I think that's still a store, right?"

"I think so," I said. "But I'm still trying to piece together the high school thing. Y'all went to high school together?"

"There's only the one high school, Constance. She was only a few grades older than me."

"That makes sense. In my head, I guess I was picturing something more like where I went to school. I went to school with my neighbors and didn't even know their names. We didn't run in the same circles. Not like you and Trish did."

Summer turned her head, scowling. "We were both cheerleaders."

I almost slammed on the brakes. And I did slow down. "What?"

"She hasn't told you?"

"Let's just assume she hasn't. What's this about Trish being a cheerleader?"

"She wasn't always Miss Doom and Gloom. In high school, she was pretty cute. I mean, I guess she still kind of is in a way. You know what I mean. She was tiny—skinnier, the same height. She was the perfect flyer."

"So, did y'all have a falling out or something?"

"It does involve falling," Summer said. "I was a spotter. You know how it works? She gets held by the bases, and I help too. But I kind of called the shots during a stunt.

"Well, there was this one stunt. And let's just say it didn't go very well. She fell and broke her arm. She claims it was my fault."

"Was it?"

Summer shrugged. "Partially. But she lost her spot after that. She didn't even cheer her senior year. I don't think she'd own up to it, but she blames me."

"I don't think she'd own up to ever being a cheerleader. I'm having trouble picturing any of this."

"I can always bring over a yearbook."

I laughed. "Maybe when I have less reading to do."

"Oh, yeah. Your grandmother has me reading a lot too. I'm worried about her, by the way."

"Who? Gran?"

"Yeah. She's been rather cryptic lately."

"She's always cryptic."

"Not like this. She's giving stuff away. She wants me to take her cats."

"Okay. That is a little weird. I'll talk to her."

Summer nodded. "Thanks."

I made the turn from the highway down a single lane drive.

Rosemary's Antiques was out in the middle of nowhere, in the farmland between town and the vineyard, a few miles away. And it wasn't painted to look like a barn. No, it had really been one. Square in the middle of a pasture, it was a red building with white trim on the doors and shutters.

"Have you ever been here?" Summer, being a lifelong resident of Creel Creek, had to have come here at least once. Right?

"Not here." She shook her head. "I've been antiquing. Usually, we go to Charlottesville. There's a lot more selection. Remind me again why you need me here. Aren't you just dropping off a necklace?"

"Yes. But I'd like to learn a little about its history. I want to know where the magic in it came from."

"I'm still not exactly tracking why I'm necessary."

"Summer," I leveled with her, "you're a reporter. You ask questions for a living. If anything, I'm the one who isn't necessary."

"I get it." She rolled her shoulders, dusted off her shirt, and stepped out of the car with flawless posture. The only thing missing was a microphone in her hand.

I smiled to myself, then thought better and frowned. I was almost as good at manipulating people as Gran—and that wasn't a good thing.

INSIDE THE ANTIQUE SHOP, it was sweltering—and so muggy it made it hard to breathe. Whatever modifications that had turned this barn into a storefront didn't include central air. Nor did they include ample lighting. Most of the light came from windows—the few there were.

A chime on the door marked our arrival.

"I'll be right with you," a woman's voice called out from somewhere in the recesses of the store, behind the sea of antique goods.

Or maybe it wasn't a sea exactly. Maybe the antiques were the land, and the narrow passages between them were streams and rivers. Either way, I was afraid of venturing too far inside and accidentally knocking something over with a stray elbow or hip.

The store was absolutely jam-packed with stuff. Tables and chairs. All kinds of furniture. Most held knickknacks and bobbles. Shelves lined the walls and went up nearly as high as the ceiling—being a barn, that was between ten and twelve feet.

Summer was unfazed by any of it—the heat or the cramped space. She began looking around, feigning interest or possibly exhibiting the real thing. I couldn't tell.

I made my way to a neat little office inside of an old stall. There was a desk stacked with receipts and an old register. Like everything else in the store, it looked to be at least fifty years old.

The same could be said for the woman who appeared amidst the items. She was at least fifty, but I couldn't guess an exact age. She was short and razor thin. Her big brown eyes matched her pixie length hair. A lot like her hair, the woman was spritely, a blur as she moved from one end of the shop to the other to greet us.

"What can I do for you girls today?" She swayed back and forth, waiting for either of us to answer. Summer had ventured nearly halfway through the barn and was preoccupied with an oil lamp. I could only hope there wasn't a genie inside. I had enough to deal with for one episode of Catastrophes with Constance.

"I actually have something for you," I told her, waving from the makeshift office. "Are you Ellen?"

"That's me." She smiled a toothy smile and made her way over. "You must be the woman the sheriff called about. The one who found the necklace."

Momentarily, I was taken aback. Dave hadn't mentioned

telling this woman I found it. It made sense. How else was he supposed to explain it? He couldn't tell her about the ghoul, not unless she was paranormal.

From what I could tell, she wasn't. Or at least, she wasn't a shifter or a witch. She didn't have the telltale signs of being a vampire either. Granted, there aren't many—vampires aren't ghostly pale. And they don't sparkle.

Ellen could still very well be different. Like many residents of Creel Creek, there was a chance she had Fae blood. A solid chance, given everything I'd noticed about her. Not that she would know anything about it... or believe me if I told her.

"I'm Constance Campbell. It's nice to meet you."

I hoped she didn't notice my hesitation, but her face soured almost immediately. "Cutting it a little close, aren't you? I close shop in fifteen minutes."

"This shouldn't take long." I dug the necklace out of my purse. "Dave—I mean Sheriff Marsters—thinks this might've been stolen from here."

"I don't know." She yanked it from my grasp and held it up to the light from the window. "This could be one of the items. Looks like it's lost a bit of luster."

"Maybe." I shrugged. "I wouldn't know. This was how we found it."

"May I ask *where* you found it?" I noticed a hint of accusation in her tone.

"I, uh—" I was at a loss, not having prepared a lie of any kind—good or bad.

"It was actually me who found it." Summer came to the rescue, doing exactly what I'd brought her here to do.

Ellen scowled. "All right then. Where'd you find it?"

"I'm Summer Shields. You may know me from TV. The news..." She offered her hand.

"I thought your face looked familiar." Ellen didn't shake her hand. She continued to study the heart-shaped stone. "But what does the news have to do with anything?"

Summer talked fast, the words tumbling out one after the other. "Well, I was working on a story—a think piece about stolen goods and how they might be recovered. It was silly. I thought I might uncover something in our local pawn shops. But I didn't. Then I told my audience if they had anything they needed to get off their chest—anything they came across that maybe didn't belong to them—they could send it my way. No questions asked. And I would find its owner."

"And someone was dumb enough to believe you?" She looked skeptical. As was I. While a fast talker, Summer was nowhere near as competent as Trish with a lie. Trish's story would've been far more believable.

"Maybe they didn't see its value." Summer shrugged. "To be honest, I'm not sure I do either. I ended up scrapping the whole story."

"Funny," Ellen said. "That's twice this necklace has failed to make the news. The way my mother told it, they weren't interested in running a story the night she was robbed either."

"It was a robbery?" I asked.

"Oh, yes. Some cloaked figure came in. Took what they wanted and left. There was no gun that I'm aware of. But still. They had the audacity to come here in broad daylight and take what was hers."

"When was that?" Summer went into reporter mode.

"Ten, maybe fifteen years ago? I don't know. I'm sure it was in the police report."

"I wasn't even reporting back then," Summer said. "I was

at my first job, assistant producing the morning news in Richmond."

"We all have our excuses." Ellen sighed. "I wasn't here at the time either. All I know is Mother wasn't very fond of the treatment she received from either the media or the police... or the insurance. Mother didn't keep very good books. They barely gave her a penny."

I had already deflated. I was hoping the necklace was a more recent memory. And it wasn't even Ellen's memory at all.

I bent my head toward the necklace. "So, you don't actually know if this is one of those stolen items or not, do you?"

"I do," she countered.

"How?" Both Summer and I asked in unison.

"Well, it's just like the others, isn't it?"

"Like what?"

"Like the others," she said again, flustered. "Her collection. All of them were stolen."

"What collection? You said the store was robbed."

"It was." She nodded emphatically. "Of her collection. Everything in it looked a lot like this."

"Like jewelry?" Summer tried.

Ellen shook her head. "You see that rock? You see the faint glow on it?" She dangled the stone ahead of my nose.

"Not really."

Summer squinted one eye, then the other. "Oh! I see it."

"See what?"

Summer glared at me as if I was dense—which maybe I was guilty of. But I still wasn't seeing what she was.

"Here. Let me show you some others." Ellen turned and weaved through the shop as if she knew it like the back of her hand.

As I struggled behind her, the words I found were, "You have others?"

"Not as many as we used to," Ellen said. "But she never stopped collecting. These rocks—they were her passion project. Some people love turquoise. She loved these stones."

Ellen led us to a nearly barren display case. There wasn't much inside the glass. Another necklace, a pair of earrings, and a few rings. Alongside them, a few loose stones. Most were like the ghoul's necklace, dull.

But one had the orange neon glow of rocks I knew all too well—the rocks from the mine.

"Mother used to say there was magic in the stones like this. If you touch it without gloves, you can almost feel it."

I was at a complete loss for words.

Summer grabbed me by the wrist and squeezed.

"How did your mother come across these?" I asked. "Did she make this jewelry? Did she find the stones herself?"

I knew it was a dumb question. The spell Gran had put on the mine made it so a person could only go in one time and take only enough magic for themselves.

"No. Nothing like that. Mother was a collector. She spent years searching for any item made of this rare material. But the funniest thing happened. One day, it was almost like they started coming to her. A random stranger would come in and trade one in. She'd get them in the mail. It tickled her to no end."

A summoning spell.

Before Gran's. Long before. There had been a company that mined a bunch of stones. Maybe this jewelry was some of their doing. Or maybe, this is just what people did with the stones they found.

Summer frowned. "You said someone came in a few

years ago, and they stole her collection? How many did she have in here back then?"

"This case was full at the time. I'd say more than fifty items. Fewer than a hundred. But close."

"A hundred," I whispered.

A hundred magical stones stolen. There could be a hundred ghouls out there somewhere.

"Close to it," Ellen repeated.

14

CREEL CREEK AFTER DARK
EPISODE 108

It's getting late.
Very late.
The creeping dread of tomorrow haunts your dreams.
It's dark out. Are you afraid?
Welcome to Creel Creek After Dark.

Ivana: I'm your host Ivana Steak. And today we have a guest—our first guest in a long while. Please give an *After Dark* welcome to Mister Ivan Rush.

Mr. Rush: I'm imagining their golf claps of appreciation. They're like music to my ears.

Ivana: Oh, Ivan, it's a much warmer welcome than that. If the fans are anything like me, which I know they are, they're giddy to get to know you.

Mr. Rush: Giddy, huh? I'm not sure anyone has *ever* used that word in relation to me ever.

Ivana: Maybe I'm the first of many. Can you tell our listeners—and our viewers over on ParaTube—a bit about yourself?

Mr. Rush: Well, let's see. You covered the basics. My name. I'm originally from the Midwest. But I've lived all over. You're probably not interested in my age or what my college degree was in—it was literature. Don't ask me what you're supposed to do with a literature degree. I'm still unsure. Oh, and I'm a wizard. I guess I probably should've started with that.

Ivana: You're right. I do think our audience would be *most* interested in the wizard thing. Not that we don't love our literature. *Dracula. Frankenstein.*

Mr. Rush: *Cujo.*

Ivana: I was thinking classics. But sure, *Cujo*. Can you walk us through what it entails—being a wizard, I mean. Are you an entertainer? Do you work kids' parties? That kind of thing?

Mr. Rush: Unfortunately, I'm not an entertainer. But I always love a good close-up magician. Card tricks. Coin tricks. I applaud those guys—the ones who have lighter fluid up their sleeves. But it's not the type of thing I do.

Ivana: What *do* you do?

Mr. Rush: Magic.

Ivana: Like real magic?

Mr. Rush: That's the idea, yes.

Ivana: Can you do some magic for us? Here, on the show?

Mr. Rush: I like you, Ivana. You're to the point.

Ivana: Why am I sensing a but?

Mr. Rush: Wow...and you're clairvoyant.

Ivana: Stop it. I thought you said you were going to show us magic?

Mr. Rush: I said I was going to show *you* magic. Listen. Nothing I do here now is going to impress your audience. It would be nothing but parlor tricks to them. And real magic isn't throwing fire from your fingertips—though I have thrown fire from my fingertips.

It's not about illusions. It's not about turning invisible. Though some practitioners can do that. It's not about stopping time. Or turning a child into a toad.

Ivana: Have you done that?

Mr. Rush: No! Well, maybe. Just once. Kidding. I'm kidding. The point is, if you want those kinds of things, watch a movie. Do you really want to see magic, Ivana? Real magic?

Ivana: My answer is a resounding yes.

Mr. Rush: All right. But I warn you. This won't mean anything to those cameras. And honestly, it might hurt. It might hurt you.

Ivana: In what way?

Mr. Rush: Not physically—if that's what you're worried about.

Ivana: You won't tell me what you're going to do?

Mr. Rush: It would ruin the surprise.

Ivana: Fine. Go ahead then. Do your worst.

Mr. Rush: It's not that kind of magic.

Ivana: Oh... Oh! Mister Rush, I'm not sure what to say now.

Mr. Rush: An apology would be nice.

Ivana: Okay. I do want to apologize—for everything that happened at After Dark Con. I'm sorry that I didn't remember you were there.

Mr. Rush: You didn't remember I was there because I didn't want you to. It's that simple.

Ivana: How did you—

Mr. Rush: Magic. I told you. The cameras wouldn't pick it up.

Ivana: But how do I know that what you did is magic? I

don't understand it. That memory—it just popped into my brain.

Mr. Rush: Again, magic. I'm trying to make it simple for you.

Ivana: I guess so. It *is* simple. Too simple, really. Folks, I can't explain it well. But for the last several months, my memory of the whole bird incident was murky to say the least. Particularly murky when I thought about the people who were on the stage at the time.

Mr. Rush: The others who attended, their memories are murky as well. They'll understand. Or some will.

Ivana: That whole thing got away from us. Again, I'm sorry, Mister Rush. We never meant to—

Mr. Rush: The past is the past. Let's not carry it around with us anymore. I get it. I've had my own plans go sideways.

Ivana: You have?

Mr. Rush: It's nothing I want to talk about right now.

Ivana: You were a lovely guest, Mister Rush. I'd love to have you back again sometime.

Mr. Rush: Thanks for having me. I'm available next week, if you want me.

Ivana: You know what? I think we do. Stay tuned for next week's episode with Mister Ivan Rush.

15

GRIMOIRES

The next few days were busy. Work was steady. The coffee flowed and the books, well, they got a little dustier. All the while, the thought of going up against a hundred ghouls plagued the back of my mind.

Not that there had to be a hundred. Trish reminded me that ghouls didn't just show up to the party. Someone had to invite them.

It wasn't clear if that meant individual summonings—one for every ghoul. Maybe the person responsible could metaphorically drop a thousand leaflets into the shadow realm like that nerd in *10 Things I Hate About You* inviting the whole school to crash Bogey Lowenstein's party.

In the hours after work, Slate had taught us spells to secure the portals. Much like a home security system, they didn't do much to protect the world. They would notify us if an unwanted visitor came out of the shadow realm. We might even get a picture of what it was and the direction it went in.

The onus was on us to react, if and when the spell discharged.

Ghouls weren't the only thing eating up my time. There were preparations with Brad and a few long conversations with Dave, who wasn't excited at the notion of letting a demon loose on the world.

I hadn't even had a chance to crack open the weird book from the Faction. Nor had I talked to Ivan.

While the Faction's leader was off gallivanting with Jade, as her alter ego Ivana Steak, Jade's former cohort was attempting to learn magic. Summer's red car zoomed out of the driveway as I pulled up with Gran's weekly grocery delivery.

It was Friday, ahead of my long weekend. I'd taken time off work, and I was trying to knock out every chore I could, so I could focus on what was ahead—allowing Custos to set a non-bound foot into our world.

But that was tomorrow's problem. I still had several hours before sunset, and more importantly, the Moon's rise.

"Hello. I come bearing gifts." Again, I walked into what seemed like a vacant house. Gran's recliner was empty. So was the kitchen table, where I relieved myself of my burden of plastic bags.

A sudden movement from the cat door caught my eye. "You bring the good stuff?" Stevie asked hopefully. "Was the canned food on sale?"

"It wasn't on sale. It's hardly ever on sale. But I bought a few."

"By all means, don't go out of your way for me."

"I never do."

"And herein lies the problem."

I rolled my eyes and rummaged through Gran's drawers for the can opener, wondering what I ever did to deserve the sass.

It came at me from every angle—including the stairs. "What's that you brought?"

"Groceries?"

Gran trudged into the kitchen. She frowned at me, unimpressed. "Those books on my recliner." Canned cat food wasn't the only thing I'd brought.

"Right...those."

"Are those spell books? You haven't brought back the family grimoire, have you? You know I gave it to you because I was tired of looking at it. That, and I know it by heart."

"Neither one is ours," I said. "But I'd like you to take a look at them."

She considered. "Make me some coffee, and I'll think about it."

"Seriously?"

"Isn't that what you do all day anyway?"

"It is. And you're asking me to do it for free."

"You used to make me coffee all the time."

"I lived here." It wasn't worth the effort to argue. At least not about coffee. I had other issues I wanted to discuss. "Hey...I have a question for you."

"Don't you always?"

"Gran!"

"It's the truth. Why do I always get crap for speaking the truth?"

"Everyone does." I sighed. Again, it wasn't worth the effort. "Did you know about the antique shop? Rosemary's or whatever. They collected stones of, um, value."

Gran answered my question with one of her own. "Whose funeral do you think I was at the other day?"

"Oh." Well, at least that mystery was solved. "So, it was you who put a summoning spell on the shop?"

She nodded.

"Why though?"

"Because the magic wouldn't allow me to do it here." Gran headed for her chair, her feet scuffing on the floor. "Trust me on this one. I tried."

Magic.

It was opinionated. It was the reason I had to make coffee. I couldn't just utter something under my breath like,

> "Grind the beans, make some steam.
> Drip through a bewitching brew.
> Black and hot.
> Make a pot.
> A cup for me. A cup for you."

The coffee maker flipped on of its own accord, and a gorgeous liquid began dribbling out into the pot.

So opinionated.

"Why try?" I turned to Gran. "Why worry about those stones at all?"

Gran settled in her chair and put her feet up. Content with his meal, Stevie padded over to the couch and curled up. I brought the coffee to the coffee table and took a seat beside him.

Then Gran did something unexpected. With a few words and a twirl of her finger, she put her familiar to sleep. I'd seen her do it before, but I wasn't expecting it.

"That was far too much stone talk for his ears. I wanted those stones out of circulation—or at least somewhere I could keep an eye on them."

"I thought you—we—were tasked with... protecting the mine." Now that Stevie was out, I could say the word. But Gran was right—I'd been far too loose with my words and thoughts.

"It's all the same," she spat. "I wanted to see where they went. Those lost stones had to be somewhere. And I was right. They were somewhere. Right here in town. Rosemary had been collecting them for years."

"So, they stayed there?"

She nodded. "For a long while, they went nowhere…"

"Until they were stolen," I finished her sentence.

"Best laid plans."

"That mirror." I glanced at the stairs. "Did you use it to spy on Rosemary—on the store?"

"One of its many uses. Why do you ask?"

"You didn't happen to see who stole that jewelry, did you?"

"He didn't show his face," Gran said. "But I remember his voice. His cold and calculating voice. He told Rosemary not to move. And she didn't move a muscle. It was almost like a spell."

"Maybe it was."

"Maybe." Gran took a sip of coffee, then studied the books I'd brought. She opened the first. "Is this what I think it is?"

"It's Nell Baker's," I said. "It has the spell to call and bind Custos."

"And that surprises you?"

"No." I shrugged. "I guess it makes sense. That's how Hal must've found it. But a lot of these spells—they're in your grimoire. Our grimoire."

"Your grimoire," Gran corrected. "And that shouldn't surprise you either. Grimoires are like online recipes. A bunch of drivel around a simple set of instructions. The ingredients stay the same. Magic is magic. It's the instructions that vary."

"That makes sense, I guess. There's actually more to her

spell. I'm guessing it's how Hal trapped Brad in the shadow realm. There's just one thing I don't get."

She raised her eyebrows. "And that is?"

"It says you need a piece of the familiar to do it—to trap them. What does that mean, a piece? Like blood or something?"

"It could be." Gran mulled it over. "A familiar might bleed on Earth. They won't die though. Their bodies are mere vessels."

"So how did Hal get Brad's blood?"

"I don't think he did," she said. "I'd wager it's more abstract. A piece of him," she repeated. "It could be as simple as his name."

"Brad?"

"His *real* name," Gran said.

"Oh." I remembered when Brad had told us his name. His true name. It sounded like metal on metal and a mixture of too many languages to count.

Hal had already hexed my phone at that point. So, it was possible he learned the name simply by eavesdropping.

Maybe, after a lot of practice, Hal was able to speak Brad's true name.

Gran set down her coffee. "You're still going through with this thing tomorrow, aren't you?"

"I don't have much choice."

"There are many roads that lead to Chicago. You don't have to take Route 66. You do it because it's the easiest... And they talk about it in the movies."

"You have a better idea of how we keep Beruth captive?"

"You trade one demon for another. They're both bad news."

"He'd take Brad again. That was another part of the deal."

"Only if you let him. Maybe we should study this spell. We can find a loophole."

"You study the spell. I've got other things I've got to do."

"Like read this other book?" Gran took its measure by twirling her finger above it. "What is it?"

She tried to open it. Like it did for Dave and Trish, it refused to budge.

"The Faction?"

I nodded.

Unsatisfied, Gran stroked her finger down its spine, muttering a spell. She frowned and carefully tried to pry the book open. "It's a nice spell they've put on it."

"Allow me." I opened the book for her, and she flipped a few pages. "What do you think it is?"

Her lips puckered like she was eating sour candy. "Constance," she said, "I can't read the words on those pages."

"I figured as much."

"Sorry." She didn't sound sorry. "It must be for Faction eyes only. Maybe it's another grimoire. They're so popular nowadays."

"I thought they were rare."

"Not rare at all. Quite the opposite really."

I showed my skepticism. "If that's true, then why'd you make it a big to-do giving me yours?"

"They're family heirlooms. That, in and of itself, is enough to make them something special. That's why they're sought after. Usually, a grimoire stays in the family. To see one out in the wild, like Nell's, means that witching line didn't continue."

"I concede your point," I said. "It makes me kind of wish I kept more of Dad's stuff."

"Oh, honey. You made the right decisions there." She smiled. It was the first time I'd seen her smile in a while.

"You think so?" I took the Faction's book and left Nell's grimoire in her trustworthy hands.

"Trust me," she said. "You never would've used those golf clubs."

I smiled and headed for the door. There was still light outside, but it was growing darker by the minute.

16

IN WITCH I STRUGGLE

When I was younger—much younger—I'd attend the midnight release parties and get the new Harry Potter novel the night it came out. Then I'd stay up the rest of the night reading it.

I was a zombie for the next few days, but at least I didn't have to worry about spoilers.

At the time, I identified with Hermione, who spent most of her leisure time in the Hogwarts library. I remember thinking how silly it was that Harry and Ron went to a magical school but instead of actually learning magic, they'd get caught up in mysteries or worse—quidditch.

The pair didn't do their reading. They scraped by copying Hermione's homework. And lucky for them, the end of term exams were almost always canceled because of their mischief.

That was then—when magical study was theoretical. What I didn't know was how dull magical texts really are. And it wasn't like I had much time to spare on study.

Like for those two-thirds of the Golden Trio, my magical learning came in firsthand experience.

That didn't mean I wasn't going to try. I had the Faction's book propped on my lap almost the whole night. It was just impossible to focus.

When Dave's Uncle Hairy came to visit, it meant a couple of nights alone with his girls. We had slumber parties—game nights and movie nights.

I took the opportunity to introduce the girls to the classics. Not *Pretty in Pink* or *Sixteen Candles*. They weren't ready for John Hughes yet. We watched 80's paranormal comedies —*My Best Friend's a Vampire*, *Teen Wolf*, and my personal favorite, despite its cringeworthy rap battle, *Teen Witch*.

Add summer break to the mix and bedtime fell somewhere between late and really late. It was close to midnight.

The littlest, Kacie, had been glued to my hip all night. She was close to passing out but managed to rouse herself every ten minutes or so. The older two had their own issues. They'd been bickering constantly since Dave left.

As we finished our light-hearted movie marathon, all three were craving a midnight snack.

Two steps into the kitchen, I realized if I was going to make a go of reading, I needed to eat something too—and put on a pot of coffee. I doled out some cookie dough on a baking sheet and popped it in the oven.

Several minutes later, cookies baked and the movie over, I returned to the living room to find the mood had suddenly turned serious.

I could tell because the older two were staring at me as if they had something to say—like they needed to get something off their chests.

Kacie fought sleep, blinking as I curled up next to her on the couch.

I bit into a cookie, waiting for either girl to say something. They didn't.

"What is it?" I asked.

"Constance," Elsie said softly, "can we talk?"

Elsie was the middle child. She favored her mother. Her hair was lighter than the other girls'. Her front teeth had grown in. They looked bigger than all the rest.

Licorice, her black cat, lay across her lap like a belt. She stroked the cat absentmindedly.

Allie, the oldest, hugged a pillow. She looked sad. She probably knew what Elsie was going to say.

I wondered if I'd done something wrong. Or said something wrong. Sometimes, it felt like just being here—and not being their mother—put me in a bad spot.

Maybe I'd chosen the wrong movies. They made light of what could be considered heavy topics in a *real* paranormal household.

"What's up, kiddo?"

"I...I don't want to be a werewolf. I want to be a witch like you—like her."

That was it. The movies. I'd shot myself in the foot. I should've gone with Michael J. Fox last. I mean, after all, I wanted to be a werewolf after seeing *Teen Wolf* for the first time.

But I could see the downsides.

This wasn't totally unexpected. Elsie loved magic. I knew that. I allowed her to be my little protégé because it was cute. When she played make-believe with her sisters, she was often a witch. No matter the game, she was a witch. And thanks to some craziness last winter, she had her own black cat.

I never thought about the consequences of these things. How they added up. It wasn't like choosing an occupation, wanting to be the president or an astronaut. Sure, becoming either was near-impossible, but it wasn't impossible.

My cousin JB had always set his sights lower. Always the same answer. When my aunt told people he wanted to be a sanitation worker, he'd scowl and say, "No, Mom. I'm going to be a garbage man."

And he could've been a garbage man—a sanitation worker. Easily. He could've been a doctor. Or a firefighter.

Elsie could be any of those things as well.

She couldn't be a witch.

"I'm not sure that's possible, sweetheart." I wanted to give her the biggest hug, but Kacie had fallen asleep on my shoulder. She was a thousand pounds of immovable object in a much smaller package.

"Why not?" Elsie asked sadly.

"Well, because your dad and your mom—"

"I know—I know about them being werewolves. I know I'm supposed to be a werewolf." She lifted her chin. "Can't *you* do something?"

"You mean using magic?" I asked.

She nodded. Her sister, Allie, reached out her hand. Allie looked equally downcast. There was only a hint of *I told you so* in her dark brown eyes.

"It's not that easy," I said. "Besides, you've seen what happens when I do magic. It's not easy. And it definitely hasn't made my life any easier."

Allie stretched, allowing her couch pillow to fall and hit Elsie, who scowled. "See...I told you."

There it is.

"I don't care what you say. Constance can do anything."

"Not true," Allie said. "Not every spell works, right, Constance?"

"Right," I agreed. "How do you feel about it?" I asked her. "The whole werewolf thing?"

The older girl shrugged. "I'm resigned to it."

"Those are some big words."

"It's what Aunt Imogene says when we talk about it. Besides, she says it's not so bad being a wolf."

Elsie didn't seem to agree. "That's not true. She said it's like being on two cycles. Whatever that means."

"Eek." I grimaced. "Well, I'm glad you talk to your aunt about this stuff. What does Imogene think of you wanting to be a witch?"

"Elsie won't talk to her about it."

"I wanted to talk to Constance first."

"And Constance said exactly what I already told you she would." Allie yanked a cookie from the plate and put the whole thing in her mouth. Chewing, she said, "You can't become a witch. You're a werewolf. That's that."

"When exactly will you make the change?" I asked her. "Do you know?"

"Sometime after puberty." She looked away. "Sometime soon."

"What's puberty?" Kacie roused awake, yawning.

"It's nothing you need to worry about just yet."

Allie picked up the pillow again and chucked it across the room at her little sister. "Wake up and go to bed."

"That doesn't make any sense," Kacie argued.

"It does. Constance doesn't want to carry you to bed again!"

"I don't mind." I smiled, thanking Allie for at least trying to stick up for my forty-one-year-old back. "I'll carry you to bed in just a second."

Allie leaned over and took Licorice from Elsie's lap. The cat went completely limp in her hands, resigned to the change in ownership.

"Plus," she said, staring into the cat's yellow eyes, "you

wouldn't get any magic until you turned forty. That's a long time."

I arched my forty-one-year-old back. "Are you calling me old?"

"No. No." She winced. "I was pointing out how numbers work."

We both laughed.

But my smile faltered because, in Elsie's eyes, there were tears.

My heart sank. There was no winning. "Elsie, what do you want me to say?"

"Nothing." The pretty little girl looked down at her empty lap. Tears streaked down her red cheeks. Her eyes were so full of them.

I had to say something. I had to make it right, even if I didn't know how. "Tell you what. Next time I see Mother Gaia, if I ever do, I'll ask *her* what *she* can do about it."

"You will?" Elsie perked up immediately.

"I will."

Why do I make promises like this?

You can't help being you. You're kinder than any witch I've ever known. Brad's thoughts filtered in from the garage.

You haven't known many witches.

He ignored me.

Even though I'd set the spells on the portal outside, there was still concern that an already freed ghoul might show up on our front porch.

I sent the girls to bed with Kacie playing possum on the couch. I scooped her up and labored up the stairs.

"And you," I whispered. "What do you think about being a wolf?"

"Rawr!" Kacie growled and snapped playfully at the air.

"That's what I thought." I smiled.

She was fast asleep as soon as she hit the bed.

Also, what I thought.

17

THE BOOK OF SECRETS
SECRETS LIE WITHIN THESE PAGES.

Secrets meant to be kept.
Secrets meant to be forgotten.

You have been chosen.
Guard our secrets. Guard our world.
Learn from our triumphs <u>and</u> our mistakes.

Within this book, you won't find secret spells or potions.
You'll find secret words.
Secret secrets.
Entries from every secret keeper our faction has enlisted.

Trust your instincts.
Our best kept secret is <u>you</u>.

Goosebumps covered pretty much every inch of my skin—from my forearms up to my shoulders and neck, then down again.

I closed the book and sat up straight in bed.

I had another few hours until the sun came up. Hours meant for sleep. After reading those first few lines, sleep didn't seem likely. My brain wasn't wired that way.

Even if I closed my eyes for the remainder of the night, my mind would be on. I'd be lucky to get an hour while it whirred.

The house was quiet. So quiet, it made my ears ring. The girls were tucked away. There was no Dave beside me in bed. No Brad either.

He was off preparing for tomorrow. I should be too. I needed rest. In a few short hours, I had to let out a demon and be ready for all that entailed.

I dove back into the book anyway.

And I found that first page gone, replaced by a tidy little scrawl—so small I could barely read it. It was the writing from the Faction's first secret-keeper.

I read how the Faction was formed. And why.

The Faction was formed out of necessity—back when magic was rampant in the world and its practitioners did as they pleased. Whole villages went missing when spells went awry. Vampires killed in broad daylight. Werewolves stole farm animals, which wouldn't be so bad if they weren't found naked the next day nearby. And often killed.

Our world had to be hidden.

Having the secret confirmed did nothing for me. It was a lot like the government neither confirming nor denying the existence of UFOs—until they confirmed. It was a secret we already knew.

I closed the book again, blinking to clear my blurry eyes, then opened it to find new handwriting. This was even smaller. Holding the page with my thumb, I ransacked my purse for my strongest pair of readers.

And so it went. Every time I closed the book to change positions or stretch, new pages appeared.

After hundreds of years of so-called secrets, my excitement faded. It faded until I was sure sleep would wash over me. All I had to do was close my eyes for a second or more.

I checked the time. It was late-late. Nearly four in the morning.

I yawned. I closed the book. I opened it.

Again, the pages changed.

And as I closed my eyes, I realized the new scrawl on the page was familiar. Except I couldn't remember where I'd seen it before.

"Mom!" I bolted upright, and the book went flying from my chest, tumbled to the floor, and closed.

My heart was hammering so fast I thought it might beat right out of my chest. My sleeping mind had figured out what I couldn't. The author of those last pages—I knew who it was.

I jerked sideways to retrieve the book, but the linens were tangled. A large weight held them firmly to the bed. I crashed face-first into the carpet. I was probably going to have rug burn on my cheek.

I recovered gracefully enough, twisting out of the sheets and springing to my feet.

Dave was slack-jawed, drooling on his pillow. He smelled earthy and sweet, like mud and tree sap. His usual stubble was more intense, almost a fully-fledged beard. True to his werewolf nature, Dave was more than a little on the hairy side, especially his chest. The hair thinned out where he thinned out. Abs bulged as his rib cage rose and fell. There were leaves in his dark hair and at least one twig.

He didn't stir.

I grabbed the book from the floor—the Faction's secret book—its book of secrets.

My heart sank.

"No...no...no."

The book was closed. It seemed like such a small thing, like something that shouldn't matter.

But it did.

The memory of what I'd seen before sleep found me—the slanted words of a left-handed author. There was a curl on the C's. The line through each T at an odd angle.

Those were what my brain had latched onto.

Both were letters in my own name. It made sense because the only handwriting I had of my mother's was a birthday card from when I turned five. She'd written my name big and bold inside it.

Gran had a few more scraps of my mother's writing around her house. I'd never studied them—not like I had that birthday card.

For years after my mother was gone, I used to pretend the card was new. I would've sent it to myself in the mail had I not been so afraid of losing it.

I picked up the book and peeked inside. I already knew what I was going to see.

I groaned because sometimes being right is the worst.

The book had skipped ahead to the next author.

I skimmed those pages, then held my finger inside the book like a bookmark. While it wasn't my mother's secret. It was someone's mother's secret. I was afraid to close the book again and lose it.

There was only one thing I could do.

"Wake up." I nudged Dave's shoulder with my other hand.

In my frenzied state, and without even meaning to, I'd mixed magic with the words and the motion.

Dave's eyes popped open. "Huh?"

"Wake up, please." I stroked his forehead and regretted it. It was slick with sweat and grime. "I need you to watch the girls this morning."

Downstairs, the TV was blaring.

"Already?" he asked. "I thought you were doing the demon thing this afternoon?"

"I am." I winced, feeling guilty. "But right now, I need to go see someone about a horse."

"I don't think that means what you think it does." Dave opened an eye. The other was shut tight, avoiding a blinding ray of sun on his face.

"What do you mean?"

"Well," he stretched, "when my grandpa said it, it meant he was going to poop—or maybe eat a horse. It kind of depended on the situation."

"Are you serious? Your grandpa ate horses?"

"Just kidding about the horse." He smiled. "He did poop a lot though."

I shuddered. "Well, when I say it, I mean I'm actually going to see someone about a horse."

"Who?" He scowled. "And what horse?"

"You know Kalene's barn?" I asked him.

"Sure, I guess so."

I chose my next words carefully. Given the way the secret book behaved when he read it, I wanted to make sure he was able to retain this tidbit of information. "Someone hid something there."

If he couldn't retain that, then I didn't know what to say.

"Does this someone have a name?" Dave asked. "What is this something? Constance, you sound all sorts of cryptic."

"I believe they both have names," I said. "But I can't tell you either."

"Okay." He exhaled. "I'm not following. I guess I'm not meant to. This is some Faction nonsense, isn't it?"

I nodded. "I can't tell you more than that."

I wasn't confident I could convey any of it to Kalene either. But she was a Faction member, and this was Faction business.

Maybe I could read the passage aloud to her.

Or maybe being the Faction's secret keeper meant exactly that—I was the only person able to know the Faction's secrets.

The book wasn't clear on that point.

What happens if I don't keep a secret?

I wondered if I would lose the position. Would I be kicked out? Or worse?

It didn't matter, I was willing to chance it. I'd ask forgiveness later. If Kalene couldn't retain this knowledge, then I'd have to find some other way.

And I still wanted to go back to my mother's writing—if that was even possible.

I hopped into the car, holding the book in my lap with my finger securely in place. I drove one-handed out to Kalene's ranch.

Before she'd left Creel Creek, Kalene had been short and frumpy. She was still short. And a bit frumpy. But months on the road with Ivan had changed her. Kalene had become a hardened warrior.

Since joining the Faction, she'd fought vampires, a couple of ghouls, and countless other unimaginable things—things not written about in fairy tales and lore. And not because they didn't try. No, if a human saw one of these, well, they wouldn't be around anymore to write about it.

Kalene still wore her hair long and braided. It hung nearly to her waist. She'd traded her cowboy work boots for a pair of tactical black combat boots with laces and a zipper on the side.

She was still wearing them, even though she was on the ranch. And if I wasn't mistaken, she had a knife sheath strapped above them on her calf.

"Good mornin', Constance." She opened the screen door. Kalene held an old coffee cup with golden butterflies around the rim. She slurped a sip before asking, "Want to come inside and have a cup of coffee?"

"I'd...I'd love to." I still held the book. My finger was throbbing. It was going to have a red mark.

She nodded and allowed me through. "It's nothing fancy like you make. Actually, that's a lie. It's straight-up sludge. Came from an old can I had in the pantry. I haven't had time to go grocery shopping."

"Sludge is better than starting the day without caffeine."

"I'll drink to that." She brought me an identical cup.

I set it down on the coffee table and took a seat on the couch.

"It's good to see you too, Constance." Her eyes found the book.

"It's really good seeing you again," I said. And I meant it.

We hadn't got on well in the beginning. But a year in Creel Creek had changed my perspective. Kalene had never been as simple and plain as I'd made her out to be in the beginning.

I'd been blinded by my own prejudices.

"We could've used you out on the road," she said.

"I could've used you here." I took a sip of coffee and almost spit it right out. She wasn't kidding. It was straight-up sludge.

"We heard about that murder." Kalene hesitated. "And some other strange things. Like Agatha—what happened to her? There are rumors. Crazy rumors."

"Like?"

"I don't know." She shrugged. "Like she didn't die of natural causes."

"She died of natural causes." I blinked through the frustration. If I was going to tell her the secrets in the book, I might as well tell her all of my secrets. "It's just, after her death—it wasn't natural."

"It's phrases like that that make my head spin," Kalene said. "What's that supposed to mean, anyhow? How can she die of natural causes unnaturally?"

"I know. I know." I set the coffee down and put up my hands.

"You're starting to speak in circles like some *other* witches I know."

"A—I take offense to that. And B—I get it. That's not what I'm about."

"What are you about, Constance?"

"I'm about truth," I said.

"You are?"

I couldn't blame her for being skeptical. Quickly, I

checked the pages of the book and verified they were the same words I'd seen earlier. Words written by Kalene's mother.

"I am," I told her. "I'm going to trust you with *a lot* of information."

18

THE BOOK OF SPELLS

"A mine? Just full of magic?" Kalene stared at me in disbelief. "And it was under our noses the whole time?"

"Something like that." I'd warded the room, so our thoughts were our own. They couldn't be eavesdropped by any outside force—like a familiar.

But Ivan's bird wouldn't need to penetrate Kalene's thoughts; they were written plainly across her face.

Kalene's magic wasn't as powerful as other witches'. This was because of her mother's sacrifice. Rainbow Moone had bound her own soul to the demon in the shadow realm. And to keep the demon contained there, to keep Beruth from slipping back to our realm, she needed more magical energy than a soul can possess. Rainbow had siphoned her familial magic—magic that was supposed to be her daughter's.

Kalene's eyes darted away from mine. "You've known about this for some time and…"

A single touch of a magical rock from the mine could correct those years her mother had spent draining her powers.

"Kalene," I said. "You don't need more magic. You've got plenty and some to spare. I can feel it in this room. You're as much a witch as I am. Maybe more so."

She shook her head. "It's not that. You haven't told the rest of the Faction."

"I haven't told anyone."

"You weren't with us these last few months. There were so many close calls. So many."

"I know."

"Do you, though?" Her voice went cold. "We only survived because of...well, because of my gift."

Like me, Kalene had been gifted a special power by the Mother. It hadn't been more power. I didn't know what it was. It felt wrong to ask her, and she didn't offer it up.

"I'm telling you now."

"And Ivan?" she asked.

"I'll tell him when I get a chance. I came here first."

"Why?" She was still frustrated with me—for lying. For more secrets.

"Because of this." I sighed and held up the book. "It's full of information. And more secrets."

"More?"

"Yes. But these are the Faction's secrets. It's this crazy book. I think Ivan left it for me—it's like this book gives me a role in the Faction."

"What role?"

"It's secret keeper." It sounded silly now that I said it out loud. "I screwed up last night. I was reading. I was up late. Too late. And I believe it had some pages written by my mother—"

"That's amazing!"

"It would be. But like I said, I screwed it up. I closed the book."

"So?" She inched forward. "Open it then."

"I wish it worked like that. I mean—maybe I can go back to it. But every time I close the book, and I open it again, there's a new author."

"Oh." Her eyebrows drew together as if she were trying to formulate a plan. Then the light bulb went off. Kalene eyed the book hungrily. "Who's the next author?"

She knew what I was going to say. "It's your mom. And her secret, well, it's *the* secret. It's everything we've wanted to know about the Faction for a long, long time."

I AM NOT our faction's secret keeper. This book was never meant to be mine.

At one time, I couldn't open it. I couldn't read its pages.

I still can't read its pages.

But today, and probably only today, it opened at my touch. It offered me a blank page.

I don't even know how the book came to be here. The demon that's controlling my mind hasn't tried to open it. It's almost like she's keeping it safe for someone. I don't know who. I don't know why.

But the book—its magic—knows something is off. It knows something is wrong with me. Something is wrong with our order. Someone is taking us down, one at a time.

The way things have played out, my hands are the only hands available.

I think the book knows what I have to do next...

I have to tell this last secret...tell the story of the Faction's undoing. And I have to do it fast. I'm writing these words on borrowed time.

The last thing I remember is an assignment. The details are hazy. I was meeting someone—another Faction member. Her name was Serena Campbell. This was her book.

My book—the book of spells—had what she needed.

Per Faction rules, the books aren't supposed to be in the same place at the same time. Instead of showing up with my book, I memorized the spell. And I hid the book as I always do.

We met. Together, we cast the spell. And at first, I thought everything went fine. Except it didn't.

I came home with something else—someone else—inside me. A demon.

And I think maybe something happened to Serena. I'm not exactly sure.

But I do know that something went wrong. The demon isn't happy. Their plan was foiled somehow.

Maybe Serena fought back.

I plan to do the same.

Beruth—the demon inside me—has been searching for my book. She needs it, or she thinks she does. She's searched through my memory.

She won't find it there. When I realized what was happening to me, I locked most of the good bits away, including all of my knowledge of the book and the spells I memorized.

It's where I live the majority of the time—with my memories.

It's where I'll go after this.

I don't know how much time I have. Not much. Hopefully, it's enough.

On the last page of the book of spells, there are spells meant for The End. Whether that means the end of the road, the end of the journey, or the end of the story—well, I'm not sure.

But every keeper of the book must memorize these spells. It's the rule. That's the secret of that book.

These spells are for dire straits. And I don't think they've ever been as dire as this.

I think it's time for our faction to hear the end.

This spell I'll utter after writing these words, it's called The Unforming. It will unform our faction.

Now, for my other secret.

After all, what use are these pages without it? And what use is this book without the others?

The book of spells is hidden in my barn, in the stall belonging to my daughter's horse. It's hidden there with blood magic, meaning it won't reveal itself without my blood.

If you're reading this, either I've failed, and this book has slipped into the wrong hands... Or the Faction has come into power once again. Someone uttered The Forming spell.

I hope, for the sake of our world and our magic, it's the latter.

RAINBOW MOONE, 7th Spell Keeper

I STOPPED READING and met Kalene's brown eyes. I could only hope they wouldn't glaze over—that the words wouldn't lose their meaning.

She looked quizzically down at the page, then back up again.

"That's what it says?" she asked. "For real?"

"That's what it says."

"I can't read it." A tear streamed down Kalene's cheek.

"I know."

I wanted to feel what she was feeling. I wanted to read words written by my mother. I wanted to see them in her handwriting. No matter what they were. No matter what they said.

I wanted to know that secret—whatever it was.

Kalene took a deep breath. "I guess this was when she had the demon in her? When it escaped and went elsewhere—and she was lucid?"

I nodded.

I was mostly relieved Kalene could hold on to the secret. Now I could close the book.

My hope was that it would reset, and after a few tries, I would find my mother's pages.

But for the moment, I held my thumb inside it—in case Kalene needed me to reread the passage.

I could do that. I could read it again, a third time, if it meant I could be done with it. If it meant we could move on.

"This spell," Kalene said. "That's what undid the Faction, huh? How do you think it worked?"

I shrugged. "It's hard to say. But given everything we know, those who were still in the Faction—the few left—I think maybe their memories got wiped or something."

She pursed her lips. "Maybe...Maybe that's why Ivan's recruiter disappeared or whatever, leaving Ivan to sort it out."

"Right," I agreed.

"Do you think Ivan performed the forming spell? I bet it's in the register. You know. That's the kind of thing that would be in there—a spell to form the list."

"I guess. Magic kind of does what it wants."

"No." She shook her head. "I mean, yeah. That's true. But also not really. Magic has rules like anything else. These books—they follow everything I know about magic. They're like a grimoire."

"How so?" Maybe I hadn't paid enough attention to Gran's grimoire—or what she'd told me about them the previous day.

"It's like a grimoire broken into components, all of which

are usually contained in one book. We have four. There's a book of secrets. Your book. A book of spells. Mine. A book of potions. And a register, which is kind of like a family tree. Every grimoire—or all the ones that I've seen—has one of those at the front of the book."

"Wait." I stopped her. "We have a book of potions?"

"Oh, yeah. You didn't hear? Lauren has it. She joined last month."

I hadn't heard, but it figured. Lauren Whittaker was the most talented witch I knew with potions.

Although Trish could probably give her a run for her money. Except Trish would never join the Faction. She was too much of a loner for that.

Kalene sipped her coffee while I fidgeted in my seat. "Constance," she whispered, "you don't have to hold the page anymore."

"It's the magic," I said. "I'm not sure what it'll do if I close it."

"I'm guessing the words will go away?"

"That's exactly it," I said. "How'd you know?"

"Don't worry about it." She waved it off. "It's all right. You don't have to hold the page anymore."

I smiled a tightlipped smile and let my finger go. When I opened the book again, my hopes were dashed. There were no more secrets to be read. There were just two lines on a page.

These pages are yours.
Here for you to tell your story.

Frustrated, I closed and opened the book again, only to find blank pages. I did it again. And again.

There were only blank pages.

"It'll be okay." Kalene put a hand to my shoulder. She infused the hand with magic. I felt calm wash over me.

"Thanks," I told her.

But no amount of magical calm was going to help. I needed to do something. I needed a distraction. I looked out a window toward her barn.

"So," I said, "do you want to maybe find this book?"

Kalene grimaced. "I don't know. Maybe it should stay hidden. If Mom thought it was that dangerous, then who are we to uncover it?"

"Your mother wasn't trying to hide it forever. You're her blood. I think you could find it. For all intents and purposes, we're the new guard."

Kalene shook her head as if she wished I hadn't said anything. She blinked, closing her eyes a few seconds longer than required. "Do you ever feel like you're destined to repeat the mistakes of the past?"

"Not really," I said truthfully. "I believe we make our own mistakes. And sometimes they reflect others. Why?"

"I don't like making mistakes." Kalene took a leather-bound book from the end table beside her couch. She offered it to me.

I took it warily. I hadn't even noticed it there.

The leather showed a similar amount of wear as the book of secrets. The pages were the same color yellow.

When I touched this book, the similarities faded away. Magic pulsed off it. The book radiated energy. It set my witchy teeth on edge. It was like touching a hot pan with my bare hands.

I'd only felt magic like this once—when I was in the caverns of that mine.

"You found it already?"

"It was like it was calling to me," she said. "I went out to the barn to check on the horses. And I just knew something was there."

"Have you opened it?"

"Just once. I read something cryptic on the first page, and I shut it. When I opened it again, the page was gone. And so was my desire to read it. I wanted to hide it all over again."

Just like the book of secrets had done for Dave and Trish, the cover of her book wouldn't budge for me.

"Let me." With a sure hand, Kalene flipped the cover open. To no one's surprise, I couldn't read the words. I gave it back to her. "It's interesting, right? We both hold the books our mothers did."

I sighed. "Except I didn't get to read my mother's words. And you want to lock your book away."

"I know. Do you think there's something wrong with us?"

"No." I shook my head. "I think it's the situations we're put in."

"Like losing our mothers?"

"Yeah. Like that. Like joining the Faction. Like going up against ghouls. And against demons."

"Thankfully, I've never been up against a demon." Kalene laughed. Actually laughed. I'd never heard her laugh before.

"Right." I could fix that. "Kalene, you don't have any plans this afternoon, do you?"

19

WHO LET THE DEMONS OUT

It wasn't hard to convince Kalene to go with me. After everything that had happened to her mother, keeping demons locked in the shadow realm was high on her priority list.

I had a much harder time convincing her to keep the book of spells. Finally, she relented and brought it along. Riding shotgun, she leafed through the book.

I was a tad jealous. While my book boasted secrets, hers was practical. It could come in handy as soon as today. I wondered what kind of spells it contained—other than the spell Rainbow had used to disband the Faction.

It hadn't taken very long to reform. In a year, Ivan had grown its numbers from just him to nearly two dozen fully-fledged members.

Then there were these books. Who dictated we were ready to have them? I wondered if it was magic. Was it Ivan?

Weren't we still dealing with the same issues our mothers had? Except we weren't possessed by demons...yet.

As we got closer to Gran's house, a small part of me wriggled with nerves. At first, I thought it was because of Custos. But no. It wasn't him.

It was something else. Something to do with these books—the books Beruth and her counterpart had sought for so long.

Her counterpart. The unnamed entity currently residing in my mother's body.

I drove on. There was a sinking sensation in the pit of my stomach.

Freeing Custos felt more like a mistake than it ever had. And it never felt like the right choice. But Custos was my problem. He held Beruth captive for me. If I were to break this promise, he would free her, and he would take Brad back down to his realm.

I couldn't stand either of those things happening.

I parked on the road. Both Gran's Buick and Summer's coupe were in the driveway, so we could access the summoning circle in the garage.

Walking up to the house, Kalene peeled her eyes away from the book and studied the little red car. "Whose car is this?"

"You remember the mine?" I asked her. "Remember who was with me in it?" It hadn't been more than an hour since I'd told her that story.

"Summer Shields?"

I nodded.

Kalene's forehead crinkled. "Is your grandmother helping her with magic? Or is she helping your grandmother?"

"Both, I think."

We went inside to find the pair of them having lunch. Summer had brought over what seemed like all of Gran's favorite foods—takeout from numerous establishments.

Their plates held tacos, fried rice, and French fries. There was a pie on the counter.

"Have you eaten?" Gran asked me. As usual, she paid Kalene little mind.

"Not really." I put down my things—my purse, the book of secrets, my phone, and my keys.

"What does that mean?" Gran heaved rice into her mouth.

"It means no," Kalene chimed in. "She didn't even drink her coffee at my house."

"Sit," Gran ordered.

For the second time in short order, magic was directed my way, compelling me into the chair next to Gran.

"It's bad enough you're doing this with the B team," she said. "You should at least be well-fed and caffeinated."

"Did you call us the B team?" Summer handed me a cup of coffee.

"You two." Gran pointed. "You aren't exactly Trish or that Ivan fellow, are you? Your magic is as weak as this coffee you made me."

Great. More terrible coffee.

"What about you?" Kalene asked. "Are you part of the B team?"

"I'm old," she responded. It was more a yes than it was a no.

I chuckled.

But Gran wasn't laughing. Her eyes narrowed into slits and she stared me down. "I'm not sure you slept last night."

She was batting two for two. Or maybe three for three? My brain was sluggish.

"I'm fine," I lied. "I just need to check a few things in the garage, and we can get started."

"You need to eat. And drink. Hydrate."

Kalene set her own book down on the table. "That's all right. I'll go make the preparations."

"No," Gran said. "You'll make her a plate. I'll make the preparations."

"It's not necessary." I tried to stand but didn't get very far. Gran twirled her pointer finger and the magic took hold.

"Don't you worry," she said. "This is still *your* rodeo. We're just the clowns distracting the demon."

"That's not what I meant," I said. "There's really not much to prepare. We aren't binding him. Remember? I'm setting him free."

"There's plenty to prepare," Gran said. "For when you send him back. Don't worry. I've got this."

She went to the garage.

Grudgingly, Kalene fixed plates for both of us. Almost everything on it was spicy. As sustenance for freeing demons went, it seemed oddly appropriate.

In short order, we were out in the garage where Gran's summoning circle spanned a space the size of a car.

Summer and Kalene took the two lower points of the pentagram. I took a rune at the top. And in the shadow realm equivalent of this garage, Stevie and Brad took their places on the other two.

Gran stayed outside of the circle.

We were ready.

I summoned the jailer of spirits, Custos the Conniving. The spell was familiar to my lips, yet still, it left a sour taste in my mouth like bile.

Thick black smoke filled the garage. In seconds, it dissipated to nothing. And the demon formed in the center of our circle. His crimson eyes gleamed with malevolent glee.

A usual, Custos wore a dark suit. Horns protruded through the skin of his forehead. They were crusted in dark blood. His shark-toothed grin sent a chill down my spine.

It wasn't just me who was afraid. "It's not too late to back out," Gran pleaded.

"She's right, you know," Custos said. "You can back out. Granted, it'd be all too easy to take your familiar on my way back. How are you today—what was your name again? Brad?"

I couldn't hear Brad's response to the demon, but he sent thoughts my way.

He's testing the trace already.

Will it hold?

The trace Brad had linked to Custos was the only insurance we had to get the demon back should he renege on our deal.

It will, Brad thought.

I nodded, and it wasn't clear to anyone—including the demon—why.

"Well?" Custos inclined his head. "Are we doing this or not?"

"We're doing this," I said.

I dropped a coin to the ground. It bounced and flipped on the concrete floor until it rolled to a stop in the inner circle of the pentagram where Custos stood.

Silver over cold iron. It broke the magic that held him inside.

I started a timer on my phone.

"Now, that wasn't so difficult, was it?" His tone was as condescending as it was merry. "I'll see you again in an hour or so."

"In an hour," I said, firm.

"An hour. That's right. Sixty minutes of sixty seconds. Precisely."

"You've already burned thirty of those seconds," I said.

He smirked. Then a pair of sunglasses manifested out of nowhere and into his hands. He slipped them over his crimson eyes, then saluted with a finger to the forehead. His claw-like fingernails turned into manicured nails. At his touch, his horns disappeared into a smooth forehead.

With a snap of his fingers, Custos vanished from the circle.

"Is that it?" Kalene asked.

"It's not." Gran shook her head. "Now, you wait. And you stay on that rune the whole hour."

"Seriously?" Summer winced. "I would've gone to the ladies room had you told us."

"Always be prepared to wait." Gran unfolded a lawn chair.

We waited.

Through his thoughts, Brad gave me a play by play of Custos's movements. There weren't many.

He went to Paris, Brad thought. *We're following him now.*

What's he doing there?

He's at a café with the perfect view of the Eiffel tower. He's sipping a coffee and reading a book.

Really? That's it?

You prefer if he throws people from the tower?

No! I just—I don't know. I wasn't sure what he'd do with time on Earth.

Honestly, it's the kind of thing I was expecting. Stevie, too.

And he's really just reading a book? What book?

I can't see it well through the shadows. And I think he's reading it. It's hard to tell. He's still got those sunglasses on. I guess he could be pretending.

Why pretend?

It could be I'm paranoid, Brad thought. *These first few*

minutes have been easy. Too easy. Like it's staged. He knew we were tracking him. He knows we're watching.

Well, keep an eye out. There's a lot of time left.

I relayed everything to Gran and the others. Over her rune, Summer fidgeted. She definitely had to pee. Kalene was a lot more laid back. She'd brought her book—the book of spells. She stood there, reading it, barely paying us any mind.

As it stands, I thought so Brad could hear me, *we don't have much to do except—*

Wait! His thoughts cut mine off. *Something's happening.*

What?

There's someone—they're approaching the table.

Who?

You can stop all the questions. Brad's annoyance managed to find its way into my head. *I'm going to think everything I see. I can't tell who it is. They're wearing a cloak. They sat down. Custos is still holding his book, almost like he's reading it to them. Stevie, let's see if we can get closer.*

"What's happening?" From the look on Gran's face, she could tell something was up.

I put up a hand. I had to focus on my thoughts with Brad. I wasn't a good medium. "Give it a minute," I said.

And several minutes went by with Brad not thinking a thing. I put out mental feelers, hoping for a response.

Finally, I got something in return. *They're gone.*

Both of them? What about Custos? Were you able to get closer? Who were they?

Calm down, Brad thought. *Custos is still here reading his book. I still have a trace on him. The other—we couldn't see through the shadows and their cloak. They headed toward the tower. Stevie's going to try to run them down.*

Okay. Good.

We went another few minutes without an update. I stood quiet. I was afraid if I talked, I'd miss a thought from Brad.

Are you still there? I asked.

I'm here. Brad sounded defeated.

And Stevie?

He's—he's not answering.

And what's Custos doing?

He just closed his book.

I hadn't been paying attention to my timer. When I looked down, I saw fifty-nine minutes had passed, the seconds nearing the same.

It was more than a little jarring when the demon reappeared.

"Back," he said. "As promised. What an eventful sixty minutes that was too. I hope you had your popcorn." Custos leaped across the binding circle with a ballerina's flourish, tapping his toes together at the height of the jump. Then he bowed. "There. You fulfilled your end of the bargain. I fulfilled mine. And the world keeps on spinning."

"Cut the crap," I said. "Who did you meet?"

"I'm sorry." He feigned offense. "You never said I couldn't see any of my friends while I was out."

"You're right," I agreed. "It was your hour."

It ate me up inside—the curiosity. But the demon had made his point. I had no right to this information.

More than anything, I wanted to know who he met and why. Why would they speak in broad daylight when Custos knew we were watching?

Brad was right. It was a setup.

Any word from Stevie? I thought.

No.

It was all a show. Custos wanted to be seen. My gift from Mother Gaia made it easier to put two and two together.

He met with the entity—the one inside my mother.

True.

"I see you're doing the math," Custos said. "Remember our last discussion? We talked about that woman who shares your features. I thought it'd be good fun—good sport—to find her and arrange a meeting."

"Where is she?" I demanded.

He shook his head. "Maybe you don't understand. You see, right now, we're even. I did for you. You did for me. Should you need something from me again, we would have to arrange another deal."

"This is why you can never trust a demon," Kalene said.

"She's right, you know." Custos winked at her. "We're always after the bigger and better deal. Lucky for you, there's still something out there I need."

"What is it?"

He waggled a finger at me. "What I want—what I *really* want—you can't give me. But I know who can. And how to go about asking."

"Then what do you need us for?" Kalene asked.

The demon's head jerked to the side. "What I need is for you to be quiet while the grownups speak."

He snapped his fingers, and suddenly Kalene had no lips. Her jaw went up and down. No words came out. Her book slipped out of her grasp and landed on the floor. With both hands, she felt at the spot where her mouth should've been.

Out of the corner of my eye, I saw Gran's mouth quiver into a slight smile. But Gran wasn't going to like what she heard next.

"She took Stevie," I said.

Custos nodded. "That was part of the deal I made."

"What does she want him for?" Gran asked.

"I didn't ask. And she didn't say. But she did have a message for you. She told me it wasn't her who let out those demons."

"Demons?" I questioned. "You mean Beruth?"

He shrugged. "She said demons."

"If it wasn't her, then who did it?"

"That, I can't say."

"Then what can you say?" I asked.

"It's not what I can say," he said. "It's what I can do. What I can do for you."

I had a good feeling I knew what he was going to say.

"I can deliver her here. Straight to you. Easily."

"What about the terms?" Summer finally had something to contribute. "What are they?"

"For starters," he said, "I need more time."

Kalene shook her head vehemently.

Custos acknowledged her with a smirk. "It's a risk. I know. One Constance should be willing to take. After all, there's still this wretched trace on me."

"Okay," I said.

But I knew it couldn't be this easy.

Can it?

There's always a catch, Brad reminded me.

"And what else do you get in this deal?" Gran asked him.

"Like I already said, it's nothing you can give me. Tell me, though, Constance, what would you give to have your enemy here right now?"

I looked around the room for an answer.

Summer was speechless. And Gran wanted exactly what I did.

I answered honestly. "Anything."

I'd give him anything to have my mother back.

The demon's smile grew wider. "Then we have a deal."

20

HOW I MET MY MOTHER

"What have you done?" Hands still to her face, Kalene brushed her lips and the skin around them, checking everything was there and in order.

It was.

As was everything in the garage. It almost looked like a normal space with its gardening equipment and tools. Gran's Christmas tree was in a box on a high shelf. I'd never seen her take it down.

In the dim light, the iron circle, pentagram, and runes embedded in the concrete were barely noticeable. I picked up the silver coin I'd used to break the circle.

Then I let out a breath. I didn't know how to answer Kalene's question.

"She did what she had to do," Gran spoke up. "Now, get out of the circle quick."

She folded her lawn chair and crept to the door to the kitchen. Gran's gray-blue eyes were fixed on the center of the circle. It was empty.

"What's going to happen?" Over her shoulder, Summer

gave the circle an apprehensive look, then did as she was told. Her red hair was matted to her forehead.

We were all sweaty and exhausted. Holding the summoning circle open for so long had leached magic from us. And it was all for naught. We never bound Custos into his realm.

The demon was free.

"Your guess is as good as mine," Gran told her.

Kalene leveled her gaze at me. She had fire in her eyes.

"Nothing's going to happen," she said. "This is one too many deals with that demon. He lied to you. He isn't returning your mother. He made a getaway. It's that simple."

"Then why did he come back at all?" Summer asked.

"Probably to get rid of the trace. Or I don't know—maybe he wanted to see Constance's face when he told her that lie."

She's got a point, Brad thought. *The trace isn't working. I can't find Custos anywhere.*

Great. I shook my head. *Just get back here, all right?*

I felt the tug of his movements in answer.

I'd already explained what happened to the familiars. Stevie was gone.

"You don't even know if it was her," Kalene continued to rant. "You don't have any proof your mother is in any way alive. And if something is in her body, you don't know what it is. When I tell Ivan about this... Well, let's just say your tenure in the Faction—it's coming to an end."

"Are you done?" Gran asked.

"What if I'm not?" Kalene put her hands out in exasperation.

"If you're not," Gran said, "then you should turn around."

We both turned and gaped at the woman in the middle

of the circle. She wore a hooded cloak, the hood thrown back. She had mostly blonde hair and more wrinkles than I remembered.

"Clever." Her voice was all wrong. It wasn't my mother's voice. It was like the booming voice of a familiar. Almost like Twinkie's voice, more feminine, but equally unnerving.

Again, Custos had fulfilled his end of a bargain. I only wished I knew what I had signed up for. A cold chill went down my spine as the demon's magic merged with mine. It was now my circle to control.

My mother's hand tested the invisible barrier of the circle. Then she pounded it with a fist, sending jolts of pain through my body.

With the day I was having, I didn't know if I was strong enough to hold her here. Whoever she was.

It was hard to see her standing there. My mother. And yet, not my mother. An impostor.

Tears welled in my eyes. All I really wanted to do was wrap this woman in a hug. I wanted to call her name. But my mother wasn't in there.

The saying goes that eyes are the windows to the soul. It didn't ring true because those eyes looked the same to me. They were clear blue, almost a mirror reflection of my own.

Behind them—operating them—there was someone else.

A hunter?

A familiar?

I wasn't sure.

Her eyes narrowed in cold calculation. She raked her fingernails across the barrier. It made my teeth clench.

Almost there, Brad thought. *What am I missing?*

I couldn't answer him. I couldn't think. I couldn't speak.

"I shouldn't be surprised," the impostor said. "This is the

price you pay for dealing with demons. One minute, they're on your side. The next, well, the next, you're bound in a summoning circle."

"Who are you?" I found my voice. It was tentative and barely a whisper. "Are you a demon?"

"Do you see my eyes? Do I look like a demon to you?"

I shook my head. "Then are you a familiar? My mother's familiar—Mr. Whiskers?"

"Was that his name? Mr. Whiskers?" She laughed. It was as cold as her blue eyes. "No. Definitely not. I freed him to wander the world. I hope he's enjoying his nine lives."

"Then who are you?"

"You won't trick me into revealing my name. Names have too much power. For now, you may call me Morgana. I've always liked that one."

"Morgana? That's *so* original." Summer stepped beside me and grabbed my hand. Her magic mingled with mine, strengthening the binding.

"As a matter of fact, I am an original," she said. "Which is more than I can say for you. Your magic is new magic. It's pathetic. I could break free if I wanted to."

"Go ahead and try it." Kalene stepped up to my other side and held out a hand.

I took it.

She tested the barrier. This time, I felt no pain. I had enough backup. And more was on the way.

I'm here. Brad's raccoon form slipped behind the boxes, nearly out of sight.

"This is some trick that demon pulled." She smiled. It was my mother's smile—one I knew from photos and memories. "But I did give myself away. Didn't I? Almost like I *wanted* you to know my plans. Strange, huh."

With those words, the triumph I'd been feeling began to

slip away. I grasped for something solid. Something true. "You're trapped here. You're bound."

"In a way. You're right—this body *is* bound here by you witches. I'll tell you a secret though. I have little use for this body anymore. In fact, I'll give it to you in exchange."

"In exchange for what?" I croaked.

"The stones," she said.

"What stones?"

"You know what stones," she snarled. "I'm in need of earthly magic. Magic your family line has concealed for far too long."

Before I could answer her, Brad asked, *What earthly magic is she talking about?*

"The stones," she said, her eyes flitting toward Brad. "Obviously, the stones."

What's she talking about, Constance?

Morgana's attention returned to me. She pointed. "Before she passed, the old woman said you bought her out of them. All she had left there was trace magic. I need the real thing."

I realized Morgana was pointing not at me but past me to Gran.

This is confusing, Brad thought.

"I hear your thoughts," Morgana said, her eyes again on the boxes Brad hid behind. "You might as well speak them."

"So, you're a familiar," Brad said. "Like me."

"I'm an immortal. That's all there is to it. I'm not an angel, a demon, nor a familiar—not anymore. It shouldn't matter what side of a never-ending war I choose."

"Did you kill Rosemary?" Gran asked her.

She cackled again. "Of course not. You know the rules. I cannot kill a witch or wizard. I can't harm a mortal, not unless they pose some sort of threat."

"We don't have any stones," I told her.

"Lies."

"What stones?" Brad boomed. "What are you talking about?"

Morgana arched an eyebrow. "You really don't know, do you? She hasn't told you about the stones. She hasn't *trusted* you with this knowledge?" She shook her head, smiling. "Tsk, tsk."

"Constance," Brad pleaded. "What is she talking about? You can't hand over earthly magic to her. That's impossible."

It's not, I thought to him.

Gran dug in her pockets. She held out several neon stones, some attached to jewelry. "You mean stones like these?"

Morgana licked her lips. "Exactly like those."

"If I give them to you, then I'll need Stevie."

"Oh, dear. I forgot to tell you about your familiar. You see, he caught up to me. We had a nice little chat. It seems you weren't forthcoming about these stones either, were you?"

"Where is he?" Gran asked.

Something large and gray bounded into the garage. "Hand over the rocks," he told Gran. "You'll get your daughter back. Isn't that enough?"

Constance. Brad's thoughts pounded like a headache. *Why did you lie to us?*

"A word of warning," Kalene chimed in. "If you give her magic of this realm, the rules won't apply to her. She can do whatever she wants. She'll be immortal and have the powers of a witch."

"Why do you think I've kept these hidden so long?" Gran set the stones down at the edge of the circle.

"Take one," Morgana told Stevie. "With it, you can walk in your true form, not as hideous vermin."

A wave of force rippled through the air as Stevie put a paw on the rock. He morphed into something akin to a marble statue. Like the demon but without the faults—the horns, the sharp teeth, or the red eyes. His wings weren't stripped to the skin. Instead, they were tattered and broken, the feathers a neutral gray.

"Stevie. I welcome you to the fold."

The familiar took another of the rocks and stepped across the circle, placing it at Morgana's feet. Then he disappeared just as Custos had done.

Morgana gave the stone a long lustful look before her eyes went to Brad. "Do we have any *other* takers?"

I held my breath.

"I'll go," Brad said. "She doesn't trust me. She never has and she never will."

There was nothing I could do. No more magic I could perform, not to stop him or stop the inevitable. It felt like sand slipping through my fingertips.

A sinking feeling filled my stomach as my connection to Brad and his thoughts and feelings came undone.

"Welcome to the fold. What did she name you again? Brad? Almost as silly as that Whiskers fellow."

Another ripple burst through the air. With it, the magic that connected us fizzled away. Brad was as majestic as Stevie, if not more so. He was beautiful.

He gave me one last look and disappeared.

The woman in the center of the circle squatted down and smiled. She rested one hand on the floor, and she reached out the other to put a finger to the glowing stone.

There was a blur of motion, and two bodies were in the same place at the same time. Another angelic being. This one had a woman's figure, raven black hair, and she was ghostly pale.

She was gone in a flash, leaving only my mother's body, which went limp. She collapsed in a heap on the concrete.

She wasn't breathing. I hadn't prepared for this.

It took every ounce of my concentration to compose myself and focus. I slammed my hand against the garage door opener.

The owl.

I called to her like I would Brad, hoping she could hear my thoughts.

She sailed across the driveway like she'd been there waiting the whole time.

Morgana might've gotten away. I might've lost my familiar. And Gran might've lost hers.

It sucked. But we could still save my mother. We could transfer her spirit from the owl.

It was better than losing.

Much better.

21

BLOOD AND THE MOON

My mother was even more beautiful than I remembered. In my memory, she was nearing forty. She had big feathery Eighties blonde hair. This woman bore little resemblance to that picture. She had aged gracefully. I took some solace in the fact that Morgana had taken care of this body.

And vice versa. This body had taken care of her. A familiar. And not even my mother's. I had to set aside the questions pinging around my brain. How did it happen? And why?

I repressed other emotions too. And the hollow pit in my soul. My connection to Brad was gone. Just gone. A void took up the place he usually occupied in my mind.

It was kind of like the void in my mother's body. For the moment, it was a shell. A vessel. I could touch her. I could see her. I could see myself in her, more so than I ever did in Gran. But this wasn't all of her.

And it was fading fast.

The owl hooted, a low cry. She swooped across the garage and came in for a landing beside the lifeless body.

"Do you know the spell?" Gran asked me.

I shook my head. "I just made one up in the mine when I trapped Agatha's familiar in that bone."

"That's fine. Like I've told you before, spells don't have to be precise. They're about intentions. We have spell books not to instruct us what to do but to tell us what's possible. We already know transferring her spirit is possible. We just have to put it into practice."

There was no time to reflect on Gran's words. She was right.

I put a hand on my mother's chest. There were no signs of life. No heartbeat. Nothing like that. Her skin got grayer by the second.

The owl fluttered its wings in agitation.

"I'm thinking," I told it.

I knew some spells by heart. Easy ones. But I wasn't good at coming up with words on the fly.

The fly...

That gave me an idea. I scooted closer to the owl and reached out a hand. The bird danced away, uncertain of my intentions.

"Sorry...I need something from you."

Reluctantly, she allowed me closer. I plucked a feather from her wing. She wasn't happy about it. She shook out her feathers and waddled over to the other side of the body.

I curled the feather into my mother's hand.

And I made up a spell.

> "A lost soul wandering,
> a spirit unbound.
> Reunite with your body,
> at long last found.
> Once again to be her,

the person you were."

Nothing happened.

"More intent. More magic. Here." Gran squeezed my mother's hand over the feather. "Try again."

I continued my bumbling rhyme.

> "Spirit adrift, you were alone.
> Wandering lost, you had no home.
> Return to your body,
> be whole, be one.
> Rejoice in the healing,
> your lost days are done."

I'D DONE SOMETHING WRONG. Or I didn't have enough magic left in the tank.

I slumped over and cradled my mother's head to my chest. I pulled her to me. And I started to cry.

The tears came. They streamed down my cheek and onto hers.

Like magic does—like in a movie—with those tears, she stirred. Her eyelashes fluttered but not enough for her eyes to open.

Gently, I lowered her to the ground. She wrenched upward. My mother gasped, her eyes opened wide—her blue eyes met mine.

For an instant, my heart was happy. This journey was complete. Then she fell backward. Her eyes closed. Her breathing shallowed.

The owl keeled over too. Lifeless, like a bird who had smacked into a window.

Outside the garage, the sky got darker. It started to drizzle. It was as if the weather—or Mother Gaia—knew what was happening. And she was crying for me.

"She's still breathing." I could hear a heartbeat and see the rise and fall of her chest.

"She's asleep," Kalene said.

"She's spellbound," Gran corrected. "Let's get her inside and see to her."

"Kalene," I whispered softly. "Where's your book? Maybe there's something in it. Something that'll help. Look for anything that mentions being spellbound."

"I—uh—I don't know." She searched the circle, but it was empty.

"Where did you leave it?" Gran asked her.

"It was right here a minute ago." Her voice turned frantic —almost like the beating of my own heart, which had been racing since Morgana left. "I had it," she said. "Then Custos spelled my mouth closed, and I dropped it."

"Was it still there when he left?" Gran was moving boxes and turning over tools.

Kalene nodded. "I think so."

Then it hit me. "Morgana... Remember how she stooped down to touch the stone? She was hiding the book behind her other hand."

"You don't think..." Kalene struggled for words.

"She took it."

I was sure of it. My gift told me I was right.

"That's what this was really about," I said. "This was always a trick. It was part of her plan. And Custos—he was reading a book."

"What book?" Gran asked.

"If I had to guess...my book. The book of secrets."

"And what would they get out of those?"

"They played us like a fiddle," Kalene said.

She was wrong. It wasn't us, they played. It was me.

"So what?" Gran said, flustered. "What was in these books that's so important?"

I looked at Kalene. I didn't know.

"Spells." Her brow furrowed. "Just spells. It's like you said before, they aren't anything special. It's kind of the confirmation of what you could do if you had the right thing and the right timing with the right words."

"The right time—like when?" Gran asked. "The solstice? It's past that."

"There's a full moon tonight," I pointed out.

"It's more than the full moon," Gran said sourly. "For those keeping score, tonight's the lunar eclipse. It's a blood moon."

"An eclipse?" Kalene sucked in a breath. "I, uh, I did see a spell that's performed during a lunar eclipse. It'd be hard to pull off."

"What does it do?"

"You remember the spell we performed to call Mother Gaia?"

We both nodded.

"Well, it's like that one. Except it binds Mother Gaia."

This was exactly the reason those books weren't supposed to be together. I remembered reading a secret in my book that pertained to this very spell.

My conversation with Gran in her hot attic came rushing to the forefront of my mind. The Mother was in danger. This spell was at the heart of it.

Kalene was right. Her book should've stayed hidden. But unlike her mother, we couldn't hit the reset button.

And it seemed the search for my mother had actually set

this all in motion. We'd gifted the books right to Morgana. It only took the better part of a day.

I tried to think. What had I read?

"She'd need a witch's magic, right?"

"That's right," Kalene agreed. "The spell called for the magic of a witch to pull it off, among some other things."

"Then they can't perform the spell."

"Wrong," Gran said. "All they'd need is blood. Drain a witch of her blood, you can take the magic."

"All of her blood?"

She nodded. "All of it."

Getting a witch's blood is easier said than done. I'd learned not to leave anything lying around—blood, hair, or fingernail clippings. All of it could be used to do bad things.

This took things up a notch.

"That won't be easy."

Gran held up a finger. "I don't mean to be the bearer of bad news, but your book isn't the only thing missing."

"What else?" I asked.

"It's not a what." Gran checked to her left and to her right. "It's a who."

I looked at the ground—at the dead owl. It could've been the world's worst owl joke.

It wasn't.

Gran wasn't talking about the owl.

There were four women in the room—Gran, Kalene, me, and my mother. No one else.

In the commotion of bringing my mother back, we'd forgotten someone.

"Summer…"

We took my mother and laid her on the couch. Gran knew a doctor that specialized in supernatural ailments—the same doctor who helped Dave when he got shot by a silver bullet. She gave him a call.

There wasn't much time left in the day—a couple of hours before sunset. A few more before the eclipse.

We decided to split up duties. Gran would stay with my mom. I was going to tell Dave what happened. And Kalene would contact Ivan and the rest of the Faction.

The outlook was bleak.

Now, it wasn't just ghouls we had to worry about. It was the fate of magic kind. There was no telling what damage Morgana could inflict if she succeeded in binding Mother Gaia—forcing the Mother to do her will.

It was up to us to stop whatever this was from happening. The Mother was too important, to our world and everyone else's.

"I have a dumb question." Kalene looked for approval to ask it.

Remarkably, Gran held her tongue.

"What is it?"

"Does Summer's blood even qualify? I mean—is she *really* a witch?"

"Even if she's not," Gran said. "I don't think we can wait to find out."

"But Morgana could be anywhere now." With the power to slip through the shadow realm and with magic, the familiars could go anywhere they liked. "How can we stop her, if we don't know where she's going to be?"

"We know where she'll be," Gran said matter-of-factly.

"And where's that?" I kept checking on my mom, afraid she was going to stop breathing. I was afraid of losing her...again.

"Yeah...where?" Kalene asked.

Gran closed her eyes and shook her head as if she were dealing with children. Which reminded me, I had another reason to call Dave. There was no way I could keep the girls tonight. We had to get them somewhere safe.

"I'm serious. Where?"

"Think!" Gran scolded us. "What do you two know about magic?"

"Not as much as you. Obviously."

Gran scowled. "Morgana can't perform a spell this complex just anywhere, now, can she? She needs to amplify the magic. She won't have near enough with a few piddly stones."

"Okay?"

"She needs hallowed ground. She needs the witching hour. The eclipse and the blood moon."

"There are graveyards all over the world," Kalene pointed out. "And she can go anywhere she wants."

"While that might be true, those graveyards aren't like ours, the bedrock of which is the magical mine."

Kalene nodded along, then frowned. "Remind me again why she can't go down there and get more stones?"

I knew this one. "You mean besides the fact it's caved in?"

"Yeah. Besides that."

"Because it's warded against beings like her," Gran said. "Only a mortal can take a stone from the mine. Even then, they could only take enough for themselves. It's why she couldn't get her hands on any over the years. I made sure of that."

"Okay. Let's say you're right. Let's say she uses the graveyard. What do you think she wants from the Mother?"

"You heard her," Gran said. "She wants to change the status quo. She doesn't like being a familiar."

"I don't blame her." They both stared at me. "What? It's a bad status quo. Look at how quickly Brad and Stevie decided to join her."

"That's not the point." Gran stared down at Mom. She didn't want to think about Stevie as much as I didn't want to think about Brad. "Morgana's going about it all wrong. You ask for things. You don't demand them."

I smiled to myself. "Is this one of those 'do as I say, not as I do' moments?"

"Oh, hush," Gran huffed.

No matter what kind of trouble we were in, I could always count on Gran for a little irony.

Or can I?

"Gran," I checked my mother's pulse again, "what was Summer saying about you giving her the cats?"

"What about it? I'm old. I'm tired—tired of cleaning up kitty litter."

"That's it??"

"Don't we have enough to worry about tonight, Constance? For starters, I'm worried about Summer. I don't think Morgana will kill her...yet. At least, I don't think Stevie or Brad would allow it. Not until they perform the spell."

Kalene nodded. "But they're operating outside their normal rules. Who knows what they'll do?"

"Well, it looks like we know enough. We know where they'll be. And when. We'll just disrupt the spell... And get Summer back."

"I'm sure it won't be that easy," Gran said.

"Then we need a plan." My mother's heartbeat was slow. It was effort not to keep touching her. I wanted to stay here and wait for the doctor.

"We'll get help from the Faction." Kalene went to the door. She looked outside and remembered I was her ride.

I found an unfamiliar keychain on a coat hook in the foyer. "Take Summer's car. I need to get to Dave."

Kalene winced. "Isn't he going wolf tonight?"

"He is."

"You better call Trish," Gran added.

I nodded and pulled out my phone.

There was a text from the purple-haired witch already waiting. A single word. *Ghouls.*

I didn't understand how Trish could have any idea what had gone on today. Or at least why she would text me that word.

There was so much else at stake.

I was about to text her back when my ears started ringing. It was high-pitched and faint, barely noticeable.

It got a little louder.

"Can y'all hear that?" I massaged my earlobes.

"Hear what?"

The ringing grew louder still until it was blaring. I couldn't hear anything else. It was so loud, it was painful. I went to the floor, clutching the sides of my head to block the sound.

Kalene and Gran were mouthing something at me. Or rather, they were talking, and I couldn't hear them over the sound.

Then I realized what it was—and what Trish meant.

The alarm spells were finally paying off.

As Slate had taught me, I acknowledged the alarm. It was like hitting the magical snooze button. The ringing died.

Then I closed my eyes and focused on the portal to the shadow realm just outside Dave's house. I could see it in my mind's eye. Several blue traces of energy flowed out of it and down the road. I followed those traces. They met green traces from the portal at the park and continued to an intersection where they were joined by red traces. They were headed this way, cutting through the cemetery and the woods toward the graveyard.

"Ghouls," I said.

"As in plural?" Kalene asked.

I shook my head. "As in an army. I think I know how Morgana plans to protect her spell. We're going to need more help. A lot of it."

22

SECRETS OF THE LEAGUE DEN

Dave had long been silent about happenings at the League of Artemis, a secret shifter society. The league was what I'd originally envisioned the Faction to be. They had a secret network of thousands of shifters spanning continents.

In Creel Creek, meetings took place at the league den, a squatty building on the outskirts of town. It resembled a small church without a steeple, like the lodge of any other fraternal organization. And like any other lodge, there was a hieroglyph or symbol above the main entrance.

In the past year, the league had gone through restructuring, changing the bylaws and admitting not only women but werewolves and some lesser Fae with shifter-like sensibilities. They'd also raised the status of *other* shifter varieties—polecats, birds, and possum shifters were allowed to hold positions of power.

Dave and his coyote shifter brother-in-law, Jared, and Jared's mother, Helen, served as Den 1203's elders.

The members milled around the bar in the reception hall at the front of the building. It served as an event space as well as a great meeting place for guests—like me. And business here was done outside of shifted form.

I recognized Jared's mother. "Mrs. Pratt! How are you?"

"Constance, dear, I've told you several times now to call me Helen. Although today you'll address me as Elder Pratt."

"More like Eldest Pratt." Jared laughed.

"Elder Jared here does his best to be funny."

"Mom hates when I laugh at my own jokes. I can't help it. I learned from the best."

"Yes. His father thought himself a comedian. It's a dad thing, I know."

"It's a taste thing," Jared said. "My father was a Richard Pryor when Mom preferred the church lady."

"It's true. I love Dana Carvey."

He pressed a finger to his lips. "Took her ages to figure out it was a bit." Jared veered the conversation away from comedy. "Constance, you remember my sister Tori?"

His sister was short and thin like their mother. She resembled Jared, especially her nose and kind amber eyes.

I shook her hand. "We've run into each other a couple of times now but never formally met. Nice to meet you."

Tori smiled. "Same. I'm always hearing good things about Constance Campbell."

"Really?" I sounded surprised—because I was. "You're sure it wasn't some good *and* bad?"

"All good things." She sounded about as sincere as a snowman in summer. "Okay. Mostly good things."

Their mother offered her opinion. "The good stuff outweighs the bad. At least it did until this evening."

"Why's that, Mom? What's this emergency meeting all about?"

"From the little Dave told me, the witches have brought the literal apocalypse down upon Creel Creek."

"Seriously, Mom? Then why's the bar open? I can't drink when the fate of the world is on the line."

"That's the reason I opened the bar," Mrs. Pratt said. "I can't not."

"What do you have to say, Constance? Is it really that grim?"

"I—uh—"

Dave came to the rescue. "She thinks it's time everyone makes their way down below. We'll discuss this properly. There's not much time left in the day."

"Properly?" Tori's amber eyes went wide in surprise. "You mean this is a formal meeting too? There are outsiders here, nonmembers and non-shifters from the public."

"We need the room," Dave said. "Trust me."

Tori climbed up on a stool beside the bar and whistled. The room went quiet. She bellowed instructions.

"Did you find a sitter for the girls?" I asked Dave.

He nodded. "I told you. Some shifters came home for the summer."

"Good."

He led us down a hallway with the stragglers.

While the reception hall was big and welcoming, league business was done elsewhere. Given the circumstances, Mother Gaia in danger of capture, it was in our best interest to hold our meeting in a more secure environment.

Down the hallway, behind a secure door, and through a tunnel dug in the earth, the temple room was sealed and full of its own sort of magic. For instance, in the temple room it was impossible, or nearly so, to tell a lie.

The air was dense in the underground chamber, warm but not hot—even though torches and candles burned.

The stone walls held the cold and the magic. They also held memory.

Who needs a book of secrets when enduring magic will keep them for centuries?

Once across the threshold of the room, the league members took their shifted forms. The majority of them were from the big four—bears, foxes, coyotes, and wolves of the non-were variety. There were also a few cats, a possum, a badger or two, and a hawk.

The true elephant in the room—thank God it wasn't an actual elephant—was Dave. Shifters look much like their animal forms but larger, bipedal, and with humanoid mannerisms. Dave's form was much more monstrous—sharp fangs, sharp claws, and an unnatural musculature. Because the Moon hadn't risen, he used the talisman to transform. He wore the small piece of ivory on a braided leather cord around his neck, where it hid in the tufts of thick fur.

He took his place at the head table next to Jared and Mrs. Pratt.

Tori stood out in the crowd. Like her family, she was a coyote shifter. She had reddish gray fur with orange highlights. Her tongue lolled as she nodded in my direction, then took her seat, as did the other shifters.

While the Faction was making other preparations, Trish had come along with me. And Dave had invited members of the city council, the chief of police, and a few other names—some of which had lost their magical connections. But they knew enough about our world to be privy to talks like this.

We crowded together at the end of the room, without a place to sit.

After some formalities, Dave handed the floor to me, and I hurried through my explanation.

"Are these ghouls going to attack the town?" Mac, a deputy and fox shifter, asked.

"It's hard to say," I said. "They have to build their bodies once they're out of the shadow realm. I assume that's what's happening now."

"I thought you said they needed magic for that," Dave said.

"That's true. I did say that. I think they have it."

"Where they get it?"

"I can't be sure. But there was a lot more jewelry stolen from Rosemary's antiques—all of which had magic."

There was a commotion. Questions came from everywhere. Too many to answer.

Helen banged a gavel and the room went quiet. "That's enough. Constance, what do you need from us?"

"Your help," I said. "Fighting off one ghoul is hard enough. There might be hundreds. And we'll need to get past them to disrupt the spell."

"Very well." She banged the gavel again. "You have our help."

"What about the town?" The mayor took the floor. She was an older woman, dressed in a smart pantsuit.

"What about it?"

"The ghouls—they're attracted to crowds. We can't have any crowds."

"That's right. We can't." Even if Morgana's intention was for the ghouls to protect her spell, one rogue ghoul would be all it would take to destroy the whole town.

"I might have an idea." Trish looked more out of place here than usual. She was wearing a black mesh skirt and stockings—amping her witchy vibes to eleven.

"And that is?" Mrs. Pratt asked.

"We ask these walls what to do," she said. "They've seen it all. We know this isn't the first threat this town has faced."

Again, there was a commotion, the shifters unhappy about the notion of sharing secrets with outsiders.

Again, it was silenced by the gavel.

"I don't care about our secrets," Mrs. Pratt scolded the naysayers. "We have a duty to this town, and it's one we're going to honor. And for the first time as elder of this den, I ask these walls to disclose their secrets."

23

CREEL CREEK AFTER DARK
EPISODE 109

It's getting late.
Very late.
The creeping dread of tomorrow haunts your dreams.
It's dark out. Are you afraid?
Welcome to Creel Creek After Dark.

Ivana: This is a little creepy, Mr. Rush.

Rush: Please—call me Rush.

Ivana: All right. This is a little creepy, Rush. Why meet here in the abandoned courthouse?

Rush: For starters, my hotel room wasn't spacious enough. I mean, even if I was able to find a cauldron small enough, I don't think they'd appreciate the smell. The maids might not understand. What would you do if you found a cauldron bubbling in the bathtub?

Ivana: It's Creel Creek. I wouldn't be too surprised.

Rush: Maybe not you. But I couldn't take that chance. It was best for everyone that I took this elsewhere.

Ivana: Why an abandoned building? I mean why this one in particular? It's got kind of a history, ya know.

Rush: It's because of that history that I wanted to be here. There are traces of magic. It'll enhance the potion. Trust me.

Ivana: I will...for now. Listeners, if I go missing—you'll notify the authorities, won't you?

Rush: There will be no need. If you disappear after this, it'll be because you want to disappear.

Ivana: Mmmkay. Rush, you aren't doing much to reassure me. Let me explain the scene. Mr. Ivan Rush, the alleged wizard, has a cauldron full of some greenish-brown liquid. It's bubbling over a fire. Looking at it, it's off-putting. And the smell, well, it's not pleasant either.

Rush: Not exactly your mother's chocolate chip cookies. Although, your mother's cookies were oatmeal, weren't they?

Ivana: How'd you know that?

Rush: Lucky guess. Now, you told me you wanted to see magic. Real magic. Well, here it is. This is a potion. It's been brewing about three days now. It's nearly ready.

Ivana: And what does this potion do?

Rush: If you drink it, you'll live forever.

Ivana: Really?

Rush: No. That's what I was trying to tell you before—that type of magic, it just doesn't exist. That's a fairy tale.

Ivana: So, what does this do then? Remove warts?

Rush: Of course not. There are medical treatments for warts. Liquid nitrogen. And most witches relish a good wart. No. This is a love potion. It would help you find your true love.

Ivana: Love potions are real?

Rush: Love potions are real. But they don't work like you think. I said it'd help you find your true love. Not woo them.

And certainly not marry them. Not happily at least. Relationships are work.

Ivana: Regardless, this is a *real* love potion?

Rush: For the moment. Until I add this to it.

Ivana: What is that? Rush is holding some sort of stone. He dropped it in the cauldron, causing the bubbling to stop, then sizzle for a second or two.

Rush: This? This is magic. It's best I don't explain what it really is. What it does though is alter the potion. The drinker will be granted something—anything. They'll be granted their true heart's desire.

Ivana: Couldn't that be a lot of things?

Rush: It's one thing. And I know what yours is. Drink up, Ivana.

Ivana: I'm not sure I want to. It looks—

Rush: It goes down even worse than it looks. But you do want it. That, I'm sure of.

Ivana: I—uh. I'm not sure I can. Wait. What does that mean?

Rush: It means drink up. We don't have much time.

24

CREEL CREEK, AFTER DARK

It didn't take much to turn Creel Creek into a ghost town. It was dark and quiet on a normal night.

Tonight, it was even darker. Not only were the streetlamps not lit, but the few red lights in town weren't even blinking. The city council had done their part.

So had the chief of the police department, ordering a curfew to commence just before sunset.

Businesses were closed and dark. There wasn't a car on the road.

Even the stars were hiding behind a thick layer of clouds. And when they parted, the Moon was barely visible. The Earth's shadow was already upon it, shrouding nearly half of its cratered surface.

Trish locked the door of Bewitched Books and swung her knobby broom across her back.

We crossed the street to our first stop—a salon at the end of the street. It had a loft above it where the owner's daughter currently lived.

Trish pushed some magic through her fingertips and carved a rune shape in the air. She said,

"This is our warning.
Sleep until morning."

A few shifters joined us at the next intersection. More at the next. At an apartment complex, Trish repeated the spell for the people inside.

Whatever happened in Creel Creek tonight, we wanted them safe in their homes.

Like the secrets of my book, the walls didn't reveal the unknown. Rather, they confirmed what we already knew about Creel Creek.

I'd always assumed a witch performed the spell that hid the town from the outside world.

I was wrong. The magic was much more complex than that.

A light mist began to form behind us, much like the morning fog. For tonight, Creel Creek didn't exist to anyone, even its inhabitants.

We made our way to the welcome sign by the library, next to the park where Dave's girls liked to play. It was actually where I'd met Brad for the first time. The thought sent a pang of twisted emotions through me—rage, heartache, longing, among others.

Kalene and Slate were waiting there with a few Faction members who somehow made the journey.

"Ivan will meet us shortly." Slate checked the Moon above our heads. "He'd best be quick about it."

Tired of walking, Trish broke down and saddled her broom. She hopped on and hovered a few feet above the road. Every now and then, her feet touched and pushed off from the ground.

At every house we came across, she performed the sleep spell.

The fog behind us thickened.

From the trees lining the road, more shifters joined us. Other paranormal beings filed into the street. It was the antithesis of witch hunts from long ago. Instead of non-paranormals holding pitchforks and torches, our mob consisted of shifters in their shifted state, a witch on a broom minus the pointy hat, and a variety of Fae.

A pair of werewolves joined us. We were over a hundred in number and taking up the entire road.

Josh, the bright young elf we'd met at After Dark Con, glowed, lighting our path through the cemetery and into the woods behind Gran's house.

We came to a stop at the clearing, a hundred or so yards from the graveyard's iron gates. Ghouls surrounded the perimeter.

The hill behind the gates was empty.

"They aren't here," Mrs. Pratt growled. "Where are they?"

"They will be," I said. "They're biding their time—waiting for the eclipse."

"Why?" someone else asked. "They have a whole army ahead of them."

"True," Kalene said. "But on Earth, they're vulnerable. Familiars can bleed. And the only power they have comes from the stones. They won't want to waste their magic on us."

"What about these ghouls?" Mac asked. "We have to fight them, don't we? Might as well start now."

"Not yet," Mrs. Pratt said. "No use causing unnecessary chaos. They know we're here."

"Right." I hated waiting. I hated being this close to my mother and not seeing her. I wanted to know if she was still okay.

Not to mention, it meant Gran couldn't help.

"Where's Ivan?" I asked the Faction contingent. They shrugged and looked at the woods behind us.

"Something's happening." It was Slate, the tallest of all, who noticed a change on top of the hill.

A lone figure was barely visible—a shadow among other shadows.

I knew in my heart who it was. Our connection, once so strong, was broken. But inside my magical well, I found a thread still holding us together.

I trusted you, I thought in his direction.

The figure straightened. Then he walked slowly down the hill. He came out of the gate and past the ghouls.

No one knew what to do nor if this was part of the attack. They looked to me. And I did nothing.

Brad stopped in front of me.

"What do you want?" Trish sneered. Beside her, Dave growled.

"I'm here for a parley," he said. "We'd like to discuss terms. Perhaps we can come to an arrangement without any bloodshed."

"So speak." Mrs. Pratt crouched, her fur bristling.

I wanted to say something, but I couldn't. I was trembling.

Seeing Brad was like deepening a fresh wound.

"All we want—all we need—is her." He pointed at me. "We'll trade her for the other witch."

"I told you Summer didn't count," Kalene said.

"It doesn't matter," I said. "She's still one of ours."

"We won't let you kill her," Mrs. Pratt said. Dave howled his sentiments on the matter.

A hint of a smile touched Brad's angelic lips. "We won't be killing her."

"They don't need to kill her to take her magic," Kalene confirmed to the crowd. "She could give it away. But she's not going to do that. Are you, Constance?"

"No deal," Mrs. Pratt said. "We'll take our chances in a fight."

I was busy holding my breath and counting the number of ghouls, comparing that number to the number of shifters and other townspeople who'd come along with us.

It was almost dead even.

Except even wasn't good odds. There was just no way of knowing each and every ghoul's weakness. And some of the townspeople and shifters were barely strong enough to make it out here, let alone go up against a ghoul themselves.

"What do you say, Constance?" Brad's oh so familiar voice addressed me. It made me want to disappear. "What do you want? Do you want a fight? Do you want a war? Do you want all these people to die?"

Everyone was staring at me.

I reached for the resolve that had built inside me over the course of the day, from when I first saw my mother's face to the league den and the march out here.

It fizzled away at Brad's words.

I couldn't let any of these people get hurt.

As much as I didn't want Morgana to bind Mother Gaia, I didn't want to see anyone I cared about get hurt.

And the truth was, I didn't know what she was after. It could be the end of the world. It could be something a lot simpler. Maybe the Mother had some solution. She could let Morgana out of being a familiar or a demon. She could be something else.

The question was could I take that chance—risk the world so my friends wouldn't suffer?

I made my decision.

It was easy.

And it was probably the wrong choice.

"I'll go with you," I told Brad.

25

IN WITCH I REMEMBER

I fled through the protests, veering away from Dave reaching out. A razor-sharp claw grazed my forearm and sent blood dribbling down my arm. It would be that much easier for Morgana.

"I've made my choice," I yelled at them.

I collided into Brad's chest. It was like running into a stone wall. He wrapped his arms around me like a vice.

Brad waved a hand, and Summer manifested out of nowhere. "You have until the blood moon to disperse. Otherwise, these ghouls will rampage."

He tugged me away, toward the graveyard.

He didn't breathe. He didn't talk. He stared straight ahead. He was so beautiful. I couldn't look away. To think, this was hidden in the form of a raccoon.

"Stop staring."

"Why?" I asked him. "Why take her side?"

"There's a memory charm on you," Brad whispered, so faint I could barely hear it. "It unlocks when you believe you can trust me."

"Trust you?" I scoffed.

As it was, the angelic being that I used to call Brad was leading me to what I could only assume was my doom. That or I had to give up magic, thereby dooming the world.

It was not looking good for me.

I had to figure something out in the next fifty yards or so.

"I understand," he said. "My behavior today wasn't what you deem trustworthy."

"You think?"

"Constance, we talked about this."

"If we did, I don't remember it."

"Yes. That's how memory charms work."

"Who put the charm on me?" I whispered.

"You did." His grip on my forearms tightened.

"I…why would I do something like that?"

"Because for this to work," Brad said, "we had to hide it from everyone—yourself included. We knew we'd only have from here to the oak tree to ourselves. It's just enough time to remember."

"To remember what?"

"To remember how to win."

Outside the graveyard, the ghouls held their positions. But they wanted to move. Their eyes followed us as Brad steered me through the twisted iron gates

We were close now. It was dark. There were figures on top of the hill. Stevie and Morgana and one other.

"Who else is up there?" I asked.

"Custos," Brad whispered. "You'd know that, if you trusted me."

The thing was—I did trust him. Or I did until today. I thought I did.

Maybe he was right. Maybe I should've trusted him more. I should've told him everything—everything about the mine and the stones.

He was my familiar. Didn't he deserve my trust?

The memory slid from some recess of my mind.

"You shouldn't trust me," Brad said.

We were in Dave's garage, staring out at an uneventful night after an uneventful day. Like memories do, it blended into the rest. It could've been a Monday, a Tuesday, or a Sunday night after a busy weekend.

Except it wasn't. It was the night before—it was after I'd put the girls to bed and just before I read the book of spells.

How surreal for a memory to be so fresh yet so forgotten. It felt like I was reliving it, not remembering it.

"Isn't trust kind of your thing?" I asked the raccoon. "I mean haven't you been asking for my trust for, like, forever?"

"I have."

"And now I've given it to you, you say I shouldn't. Why's that?"

"Constance, I've lied to you. I've lied to everyone. But especially to you."

"I'm not following." I kind of laughed.

Brad was serious. With a paw, he scrubbed his raccoon face, then threw both paws out in frustration. "I lied to you. How's that so hard to grasp?"

"How did you lie?" I was equally frustrated. He wasn't making any sense.

He was my familiar. He couldn't lie to me. At least I didn't think he could.

"I'll tell you if you'll stop asking questions and listen."

"I'm listening." What else did I have to do? Oh, that's right. I wanted to read some of that book and go to bed. I had to let a demon out the next day. That had to be what this was about.

Brad had spent over a month locked in Custos's realm. Maybe he had lied about not being scared of going back.

You're thinking. His voice popped into my head. *You're thinking a lot. I need you to stop and listen.*

"I can't shut off my mind."

"You should learn to." He shook his head. "I knew it'd be like this. You never make things easy, do you?"

"I'm sorry. I wasn't aware we were having this type of discussion…until suddenly, we were." I paced the length of the garage, trying to clear my head, but stray thoughts kept popping up. And jokes. "Is Brad even your name?"

"Constance."

"Seriously. What type of lies are we talking here?"

"Big ones," he said. "Take a seat."

"Where?"

"Anywhere!"

It was kind of cute to see a raccoon so frustrated.

And stop thinking!

"Fine." I plopped down on the concrete, crisscross applesauce. "This better?"

He nodded, then he began to walk on two legs, his front paws held behind his back.

"You named me Brad," he said. "It's as real a name as any. But my *other* name—the name I told Stevie…" He repeated the word. I couldn't understand it. To me, it sounded like a mix of Latin and the harsh sound of metal against metal—the grinding of gears in a manual transmission. "…it's not my *true* name. It's one I was given by Mother Gaia."

"Why does that matter?" I asked. "And why would you lie about it?"

"Let me finish." He wouldn't look at me. His beady black eyes stared out at the empty portal to the shadow realm. "I *also* lied about never being a familiar."

There was nothing I could do about it. My mind and my mouth just wouldn't stop. "You lied about that?"

"I'm trying to spoon feed this to you when you want it through a hose. What I'm trying to tell—what I've been trying to tell you is I am Mr. Whiskers. Or rather, I was—when I was your mother's familiar."

My mind stopped working altogether.

"I wish I could show you what was done to break that bond. I wish I could show you every mistake I've ever made... What do you want to know?"

I struggled to answer. I struggled to breathe.

How could Brad be Mr. Whiskers?

It made no sense.

But the damn gift from Mother Gaia confirmed its truth.

"Do you want me to show you how it's true?" Brad asked. "Is that what you want?"

"No." I shook my head. "I want to know why—why you betrayed her."

"I don't expect you to understand what it's like for us," Brad said. "We live forever. We see these other lives come and go. To me, your mother wasn't anyone special. She was another witch under my charge. Another witch in a never-ending line of witches."

A tear rolled down my cheek. I was having trouble keeping it together.

This was worse than anything I'd ever experienced. Worse than walking in on my husband cheating on me. Worse than losing my dad. Even worse than losing my mom.

And Brad had caused it.

Even if it was going to make it hurt worse—explanations always do—I wanted to know how.

"It wasn't your mother's fault that I was so weary," he said. "I was questioning everything. My choice of remaining neutral. My choice of staying on Earth and not going elsewhere. I wondered what would happen if a familiar chose to just walk away. None of it mattered to me. I wanted out. By any means necessary."

The tears were flowing now. My eyes stung. Snot bubbled onto my upper lip. And my heartbeat throbbed inside my ears.

I fought back the sobs, afraid the girls might hear me crying and come outside before I got the answers I so desperately needed.

"How?" I sputtered. "How did you do it?"

"It was presented to me," he said. "Your mother was on a mission without me. She returned to the hotel where we were staying, and something was different. Something was off. Someone had taken her body—a familiar, I think. I don't even know her name. I'd never heard of or seen anything like it.

"So, she explained. She played into my doubts. Into my every desire.

"You see, there's a binding between a familiar and a witch. And she taught me how to sever that bond.

"I think this is what enabled her to move your mother's spirit into the owl."

"And you just let her?"

"She duped me," Brad said.

"What do you mean?"

"As soon as it was done, she ridiculed me. She acted as if I was something beneath her. She told me I was free. But I wasn't. I was without magic. I was without access to the shadow realm. I was just a cat. And she thought it was hilarious."

"What happened?"

"It took me a long time, lots of unanswered prayers, but finally, Mother Gaia granted my wishes. I was a familiar again. Your familiar."

"Then you met her again," I said. "With Hal."

"That's right. And she didn't remember me at all. Granted, I was now a raccoon, not a cat. She gave me the whole spiel again, offered me freedom if I severed my tie with you."

"And you didn't."

"I didn't," Brad said. "So, she exchanged me for someone in Custos's realm—I'm not sure who. I couldn't see because she and Hal trapped me there.

"It's funny. I thought it was punishment for my crimes. Well-deserved."

"Why didn't you tell me any of this?"

"Because she was still out there. She's still out there. And as long as she is, you aren't safe. She can read your thoughts. She knows how much you want your mother's body."

"So, why are you telling me now?"

"Because now you have what she wants. That book. I'm sure she has a plan to take it. And it might succeed. It might not. Through the trace on Custos, I heard her plans. Yes. They're scheming together. And I say we let them. We can use Custos. Make him think it's his idea even."

"Why him?"

"Because he wants freedom. He wants it for himself. Trust me. If we play this right, we can get your mother back."

"I feel like there's a but coming.

"We'll have to stop their grander scheme, whatever it is."

"Oh, well, sounds simple enough."

"It won't be. But at least we have a plan. But to sell it, you'll have to really believe it. You'll have to forget this conversation ever happened. And you'll have to trust me to do the right thing when the time comes to do the right thing."

26

IN WITCH I'M BOUND

Brad's grip loosened slightly. I climbed the hill under my own steam.

It figured the place I'd lose my magic was the place I'd come to know it best. The old oak tree—the massive moss and fern-ridden tree at the top of the hill—was a conduit for magical energy. Its roots dipped down into the mine.

We used the tree at every circle. Met around it, placed our hands upon it, and it channeled our magic out into the world.

Closer now, I was able to make out the figures at the top of the hill. They wore cloaks. Hoods hid their angelic—and demonic—faces. Where the cloaks hid their wings, albeit not as well as it did their faces, they appeared hunched.

Brad jerked me to a stop several feet away from the others. "Don't think about any of this," he whispered. "Remember, she can read your thoughts, just as I can. For this to work, she has to believe I'm on her side."

I nodded. I couldn't make my mind go blank, so I concentrated on the thought of losing my magic.

It wasn't so bad. I'd gone forty years without it. And the year with magic hadn't been the greatest of my life.

But what year is?

They're always filled with peaks and valleys. Highs and lows. I had a lot of highs over the past year. They were close enough to match the lows.

With a length of rope, Brad tied my left wrist, then wound the rest behind the tree. He bound the other wrist.

I was stuck there with a view down the hill to where the crowd was still gathered, marked by the bright elf.

Mrs. Pratt—Helen—was surely coming up with some plan. I was kind of glad Dave in his wolf form couldn't speak or think in the same way as his mortal form. For now, he was wary enough of the ghouls not to come charging in, but we couldn't count on that for long.

Overhead, the Moon was nearly gone—almost completely blacked out by Earth's shadow.

Clouds floated past it and out of view.

Morgana lowered her hood and looked up.

"It's almost time," she said. "It's fitting. I've come full circle. Taken magic from mother and now daughter. And next from the crone of crones. From *the* Mother."

Morgana nodded, then studied the crowd. I wondered if Brad's threat was real—if the ghouls would attack at the eclipse.

"They'll attack when I tell them to attack," Morgana said. "Do you have other questions that need answers? If not, I have one of my own."

"What?" I asked.

"Did you give your magic freely to this spell?"

"I, uh..." I didn't know what to say.

Brad lowered his hood and nodded. Then Stevie removed his and looked up at the Moon. There was barely enough light to reveal his angelic face. Only Custos remained hidden beneath his cloak.

"I give my magic freely," I said.

Something inside me stirred. It didn't hurt. It was like losing a tooth, except the tooth was part of my soul. I felt nothing where I usually felt something. And I kept putting my metaphorical tongue in the empty place.

Morgana held out a hand. She whispered a spell and a knife appeared. "We need her blood."

"We don't," Brad said. "She gave her magic freely. I can sense it."

"You didn't read the spell." Morgana shook her head "The circle called for salt and iron and a witch's magic. That's how to bind the Mother. There's no other way."

It seemed like a test. Brad was failing this test. I couldn't let that happen.

"You do it," I told him. "I'd rather it be you."

"Fine." Morgana handed the knife over to Brad.

He nodded and held up the knife. There wasn't enough light for it to even glint. I could feel though. He deepened the scratch on my forearm, collecting my blood into a stone bowl Morgana had manifested beneath me.

My arm stung. I clenched my teeth and tried to wrench away only to find my feet wouldn't move. I could barely hold myself up. It had been such a long day. I had no energy, no magic, and losing this amount of blood was causing my body to crash.

"There," he said, "this should be enough."

He cleaned the knife on his cloak, and it disappeared in the folds. Morgana took the bowl, held it in both hands, and chanted something. The blood moved on her command, dispersing into a neat circle in midair just in front of her.

The sky went pitch black for a few seconds, then the

Moon returned. It returned completely, no shadow. It was a coppery red.

The blood moon.

Morgana began to chant. I couldn't make out the words. I felt like I might pass out at any moment.

I wanted so badly to see what happened next.

I struggled to keep my eyes open.

A shadow appeared inside the circle. It resolved into the form of a tall woman. Morgana chanted louder, her words more precise. I could almost make them out.

But I *had* to close my eyes.

I hoped I'd done okay.

I trusted Brad to finish this without me.

At my thought, Morgana's chant broke off, and her eyes snapped in Brad's direction.

He had already raised the knife. Brad sliced Morgana's arm. Her blood sprayed down, in a thick line on the ground, crossing my own—the blood she needed to bind Mother Gaia.

And the magic binding the circle broke in a quick whoosh of energy.

The whites of Morgana's eyes are the last thing I remember seeing before all hell broke loose.

27

BATTLEGROUND

When I came to, it was almost completely dark again. A sliver of the Moon had reappeared. I squinted down the hill. The gigantic shapes over the fence weren't good.

Ghouls were everywhere, scattered across the clearing. Shifters and others were engaged in combat.

Below me, near the gate, a werewolf crouched low to the ground. His head swung left and right, checking the perimeter fence. Dave was protecting me, should a ghoul start up the hill for some easy prey.

I was safe for now but still bound by rope. Yanking only caused pain, especially in the injured arm. I could maneuver around the tree but only an inch at a time.

I wanted a clearer picture of what was happening.

There wasn't enough light to see much of the action. I had to judge how things were going by cries, screams, and yelps of pain. The sounds the ghouls made were equally disturbing.

Ghouls didn't breathe or moan. They moved with a sickening squelching sound.

I heard one ghoul splatter, much like in the alleyway. A good sign.

Then Josh lit up the clearing, and I didn't feel so good anymore.

Dozens of ghouls charged the gate.

Dave let out a howl, which the ghouls took as a challenge. I guess it was.

Using a barreling maneuver, werewolf Dave rammed the first ghoul, throwing his back at its side, then he chomped at the next and slashed at another.

He fought, entangled with three ghouls, until another came over the top in an attempt to smash him. Sharp claws extended, Dave punched into the ghoul's makeshift flesh. His paws plunged inside it and found the jewelry at the ghoul's heart. With another sickly sucking sound, he tore the jewelry out of its chest, and the ghoul splattered into nothing.

He managed to do much the same to the others.

Some shifters caught on to the move. In mere minutes, the number of ghouls was reduced by half.

Josh's glow was enough for me to see the clearing but not enough to light up the graveyard.

I was no longer worried about ghouls. I wondered where everyone else had gone—Brad, Stevie, and Custos. They were nowhere to be seen. And the circle that had held the Mother was a black ring on the ground.

Had they left when the spell went awry?

And where's Morgana?

Right here. Her voice penetrated my mind as a cloaked figure stepped from the shadows of one of the mighty oak's limbs. Her cold hand wrapped around my throat. The other hand held the knife Brad had used.

"Is this what you wanted?" she seethed, venom in her tone. "To die powerless and alone."

"Is this what you wanted?" I asked her. "There are easier ways to become a demon."

"Except now I'm not killing a witch," she said. "I'm just killing you."

A shape dropped out of the tree and grappled with her. Brad—he flickered from raccoon to celestial being and back again. He was nearly out of magic.

She threw him off, and he lay panting in the grass. Then he got up and climbed the hill after her. He made a pitiful attempt to push her away from me before stumbling, clutching his side. Morgana's blade was lodged there.

"Don't do it," he said to her.

"Why?" she sneered. "I've already come this far."

"Because she is my witch, and it's my duty to protect her from fiends like you."

"Didn't you hear? She's not a witch. She has no magic."

"Is that right?" Brad asked.

"She gave hers away. And you severed your tie to her. You swore it."

"No. I said it. And I'm allowed to lie."

If Brad hadn't said anything, I'm not sure I would've realized it was there. When I went feeling around for my magic, I found the thread. I tugged on it, saying the first rhyme that came into my head.

"Set me free, so I can punch her with glee."

The rope came undone, freeing my hands.

I hit Morgana with my best right hook.

It wasn't much. Muhammad Ali, I was not. It knocked her clear of the tree.

Above us, Earth's shadow on the Moon was halfway across when the silhouette of a witch on a broom zoomed across it.

Using the tip of her broom like a battering ram, Trish swooped in and hit Morgana square in the gut. They both flew out of sight, the witch back into the night and the familiar landing on the other side of the iron fence.

Somewhere in the distance, another ghoul splattered.

Just ahead of me, a woman appeared, as though she'd been there the whole time.

The Mother waved her hand, and the world around us went silent and still.

28

MOTHER TO CRONE

Mother Gaia was beautiful in so many senses of the word. In fact, there was no other word available to describe her. Gorgeous wouldn't work—even though she was. Bewitching. Lovely. Alluring. She was all those things. But so much more. There was wisdom behind her gaze.

To describe her using my own sensibilities... She was like a hot cup of coffee on a winter morning. Like an autumn day mixed with summer sunshine and the smell of spring—if those things could be wrapped into a person.

Words failed me.

I stood there in the moonlight, dumbfounded. Moonstruck.

Brad managed to get up on one knee, kneeling, his head bowed. Others gathered around—the shifters, the were-wolves, those with Fae blood, Summer and Slate. Trish landed softly in the grass. She touched her broom to the ground like a walking stick.

"Are you okay?" I asked the Mother, then realized it was a silly question.

She smiled slightly, confirming it was a silly question.

"What should happen to her?" I tried to find Morgana in the crowd. It seemed she'd gotten away.

Mother Gaia gave the slightest of shrugs.

"The Mother doesn't dole out punishments." It was Stevie who spoke up.

I wasn't sure how to feel about Stevie—I didn't know if Brad had brought him into the plan or if he'd joined Morgana of his own accord.

"Then we've got to find her." I wanted to search. I couldn't allow her to go free.

The Mother shook her head.

"We'll find her," Brad assured me. "She won't have gotten far. She didn't have enough magic left to last her more than another minute or so."

I nodded. Granted, I wasn't sure what we'd do when we found her. I didn't have much power. Nor did I have access to a place to imprison an immortal.

A cloaked figure stepped from the crowd. Like Brad, he kneeled and bowed his head. "It wasn't solely Morgana's fault," he said. "I bear some responsibility for this."

"As do I," Brad said.

"Me too." Stevie took his place beside the other two.

I couldn't see where this was going—if Mother Gaia couldn't punish them, then what could she do?

Custos removed his hood and looked beseechingly at her. "I have a request for the Mother, should she allow such a thing from a being like me."

Mother Gaia inclined her head. Her lips were pressed together. She wasn't happy with the demon, but she allowed his request.

"I've been in my realm for a very long time. I've been a prisoner in my own prison. If it's possible, I mean if it's okay,

I'd appreciate some sort of relief. A replacement—even if it's not permanent."

"I can take his place," Stevie offered.

The Mother nodded, and that seemed to settle matters for all of them.

Mother Gaia's eyes went to the crowd around us. They were still as stupefied as I'd been in that first second of seeing her. She smiled at them and their wounds were healed.

It reminded me. My mother. "Mother Gaia," I said. "Will my mother be okay?"

The Mother didn't answer me, but my magic returned, flooding into me. I asked the gift she'd given me, which confirmed my mother was going to be all right.

Mother Gaia walked away, down the hill toward the clearing.

"Wait! Before you go."

She looked back at me, still smiling.

"Mother Gaia," I said meekly. "I have a request. I mean, if it's not too much trouble. And if it is, I'm sorry for asking."

Again, I felt silly for asking a silly question—almost like a little girl who just can't keep her mouth shut. Much like the girl who prompted the question.

"I was wondering if maybe it would be okay for...for Elsie...to decide for herself. Can she maybe choose whether to become a werewolf or a witch?"

The Mother's face was contemplative. She shrugged and pursed her lips in the way a reluctant father might.

She glided down the hill. But when she got to the gate, someone was blocking her way.

Gran had come out of nowhere. She was standing there in her nightgown. "I want to go with you."

And now, the Mother wasn't smiling. She narrowed her eyes.

Undeterred, Gran straightened. She spoke louder, her voice determined. "I want to go to your realm. I want to learn from you. I want to learn where magic comes from. I want to help protect it, so things like this can't happen."

The Mother considered much longer than she'd considered Elsie's request.

Gran had more to say. "I've made mistakes in this life. Many mistakes. But I always treated magic with the respect it deserved. I'm an old woman. I don't have much else to give this world. I'm better off somewhere else. If that isn't with you in your realm, well, then I'll understand. I won't like it. But I'll understand... What do you say?"

The Mother held out her hand.

Speechless, Gran didn't take it. She searched the crowd until she found my face. Her eyes met mine. "You don't need me anymore. You have your mother now. She'll be fine. I'll see to that."

A tear fell down my cheek as I nodded.

"I did my best," Gran said. "I'm sorry if sometimes it didn't seem that way."

"I love you," I said.

"I hope you don't expect me to say I know. Cause I didn't know—I suspected but I never knew." She hugged me. "I love you, my girl. Take care of your mother. Take care of Creel Creek. I guarantee this isn't the last we see of each other. It's only a goodbye for now."

I squeezed her tightly. Around us, the crowd murmured well wishes.

Mother Gaia snapped her fingers but left her hand out for Gran.

"I'm coming. Hold your horses."

She crossed the distance between them, looking back at me one last time. Her blue-gray eyes sparkled as she took hold of the Mother's hand. And they disappeared.

29

IN WITCH THE TAPE KEPT ROLLING

Ivana: Does that bird *always* follow you around?

Rush: Most of the time.

Ivana: It's a she? Well, she's kind of creepy.

Rush: You don't know the half of it.

Ivana: What does that mean?

Rush: Nothing. It means nothing.

Ivana: You know...it's kind of strange. Constance used to have a bird. An owl. It followed her.

Rush: That *is* a funny coincidence.

Ivana: Is it? Why do I get the feeling you don't think it's a coincidence?

Rush: Because, well—hey I have a question for you. What's *your* favorite bird?

Ivana: Cardinals. Why?

Rush: *Whistling*

Ivana: Is that more magic? Did you make that cardinal appear?

Rush: Yes, I guess it is. That bird is for you.

Ivana: Speaking of magic, I don't think this potion's working.

Rush: You don't by any chance have Fae blood, do you?

Ivana: Fae blood? What's that?

Rush: Forget I said anything. In a few moments, you'll forget everything.

Ivana: Forget what?

Rush: That's the ticket. There, now...go to sleep. She's here.

Unknown: Where—where am I?

Rush: You're safe...for now.

Unknown: You!

Rush: Me.

Unknown: You orchestrated this? You helped me get my hands on those books?

Rush: I figured it was only fair. After all, it was *you* who set me free of Custos's realm, exchanging me for the familiar —or am I mistaken?

Unknown: You weren't supposed to know about that. It was a secret.

Rush: Demons don't keep secrets. That's the first rule of demonology.

Unknown: Who's that?

Rush: The raven? That's the *other* demon I summoned that day. The demon who was *supposed* to end up in Serena Campbell before you went and ruined everything.

Unknown: I ruined it? If I recall, Serena had already sent you down to Custos before I even showed up. Was that before or after that one got free?

Rush: After. Just after. I spent the better part of a year in search of her. She makes a good pet now. I might even allow her some freedom one of these days.

Unknown: What about this other bird? Who's that?

Rush: Who do you think?

Unknown: Oh...I get it. And I'm guessing you stuck me in this mortal body to prove that point.

Rush: Too right, I did. I knew your plan wasn't going to work. Still, I let it play out anyway. Look how far it got you.

Unknown: Not very. What do you want?

Rush: I figured maybe we could be partners again. If you're interested. If not, I know a bird who might like to take that body for a spin.

Unknown: That won't be necessary. What's your plan?

Rush: You're familiar with the saying 'If you can't beat them, join them.' Well, I've coined a phrase of my own—if you can't beat them, join them. Then beat them...

30
IN WITCH THE FACTION STAYS

It was a busy morning at Bewitched Books. About half the town came out in search of java juice, almost as if they'd been up all night howling at the Moon.

They traded gossip and other tidbits as the fog outside lifted.

The fog was still thick when Dave came in for his second cup of coffee. The Faction rolled in a few minutes later, making it a party.

We stood around, not really saying much of anything. I doled out coffee.

No one blamed me for releasing a demon. Or for Morgana stealing the Faction's books. Like me, they were happy to have made it through alive and in one piece.

Creel Creek had come together as a town, and we'd won. Sort of. There was still no sign of Morgana.

I sent a thought to Brad. He and Twinkie had begun the search. Dave and the local police were looking too. He sent out an all-points bulletin. But without knowing what form —or whose—Morgana had taken, it was going to be difficult to find her.

Before he left, I gave my hairy monster a kiss and plucked a leaf out of his hair.

Then it was just the Faction and Trish, who was asleep on her feet.

It would be ages before I caught up on sleep. Good thing coffee gives me superpowers.

"You did good last night." Slate leaned on the counter, so we were nearly at eye level. "Next time though, give us some warning, all right?"

"Next time?" Summer scowled. "There won't be a next time...will there?"

"We're the Faction." Slate laughed. "This is kinda what you signed up for."

"Really?"

Kalene rolled her eyes. "Normally, it doesn't get that intense."

"Not true." Slate took his weight off the counter and stretched. "Normally, we don't have that much backup. They really came out of the woodwork."

"That's Creel Creek," Trish said without opening an eye. That or she blinked for a very long time.

Slate was wide awake. "That Morgana was a piece of work, though. Makes me kind of glad I don't have a familiar."

"You can share mine," Summer offered. "He's pretty nasty. Is the name Custos the Cat too on the nose? It doesn't have the same ring as his other name. And he's still conniving."

"All cats are conniving," Slate said. "It's only right he's yours after what he helped put you through."

"It wasn't that bad."

"I'm sorry about that," I told her for the thousandth time. "My fault."

"Not your fault," she said. "I wanted to be there helping you. I had fun at the antique shop. But there's one thing I don't get."

"Just one?" Ivan sounded surprised. "I can count off ten things I don't get about what happened last night."

"You weren't even there." Kalene scowled. "I called you a dozen times. You never answered."

"I already told you where I was. I was with Jade," he said. "I was afraid she'd follow me."

"You could've spelled her to forget."

"It's cool," Slate said. "It's kind of nice actually. Like what we talked about, Constance. Ivan's always putting the weight of the world on his shoulders. Now, we know we can handle things without him."

"You did great without me. And like I said before, for whatever reason, the magic wouldn't work on Jade."

"How is Miss Steak?" Summer asked him.

"She's good. In fact, I think she'd be up for some reconciliation."

"That doesn't sound like Jade."

"She's a new woman."

"I'm sure she is." Summer didn't look convinced.

"So, what don't you get?" I asked her. "From before."

"Oh! Your gran—she said the person who took all those stones had a man's voice. Morgana didn't."

"Huh." I puzzled over potential solutions but came up blank.

"I think we better head out," Ivan said.

"You're leaving?" Even though I didn't ask, he knew what I meant. Now that the threat was over, the Faction would go elsewhere. It was what they did.

"No." Ivan shook his head. "Actually, I think a few of us

plan to stick around here a little longer. Creel Creek is a fun place. You never know what's going to happen next."

31

CREEL CREEK AFTER DARK
EPISODE 110

It's getting late.
Very late.
The creeping dread of tomorrow haunts your dreams.
It's dark out. Are you afraid?
Welcome to Creel Creek After Dark.

Ivana: I'm your host, Ivana Steak. Joining me today are my cohosts, Athena Hunter and Mister Ivan Rush. It's good to have you back, Athena.

Athena: It's good to be back. I have to say I was a little surprised when Rush said you wanted me.

Rush: It's simple enough. I told her how we got on, and I showed her a little magic. Now, we can speak from the same experience.

Ivana: I think what Rush is trying to say is the show no longer needs to speculate. We know magic is real.

Athena: But no one will believe us.

Rush: That's not true. There are plenty of listeners who believe. They're your loyal fans.

Athena: And everyone else? What about the rest of the

world? We could show them a video of the craziness that just transpired, and they wouldn't bat an eye. In fact, one of those shifter kids—they got it all on camera. They posted it on ParaTube. You should check out the comments. Everyone thinks it's fake.

Rush: That's just how it goes these days. If you show grainy footage, then people are going to complain that it's too grainy. They can't make out anything.

Ivana: If you show ultra-high definition, they're going to claim it's photoshopped.

Athena: What are you two trying to say?

Ivana: We're saying there's no winning.

Rush: But there's no losing either.

Athena: What does that even mean?

Rush: It means everyone should believe what they want to believe. The truth they're after is there, they just have to find it for themselves.

Ivana: Or take *our* word for it.

Rush: Or that.

Athena: Well, if we're going to talk about what happened—I can't believe she got away.

Rush: She'll turn up again.

Athena: I guess. It's just weird to me—the way it all went down. Almost too neat. Almost like someone else was pulling the strings.

Rush: That's an interesting take. Have you talked to anyone else about it?

Athena: No...should I?

Rush: I don't think so. In fact, I think maybe you sound a little paranoid.

Ivana: I agree. Why don't we wrap up for today? Rush, you have the honor.

Rush: This concludes this episode of Creel Creek After

Dark—a paranormal podcast for paranormal people. Somewhere in Virginia, in the Blue Ridge Mountains, there's a town named Creel Creek. There, supernatural people—shifters, werewolves, witches, and maybe a wizard—live among the mortals.

The stories are a lot like any other. They're about real people, and they're filled with humor and love. And like *all* stories, when you look closer, you can find a hint of magic in them.

Ivana: Sometimes *more* than a hint.

Rush: Sometimes.

Ivana: Viewers, listeners, it's our vow to continue to tell these stories for as long as you continue to tune in. This has been Creel Creek After Dark. I'm Ivana Steak.

Rush: And her cohosts... I'm Ivan Rush.

Athena: I'm Athena Hunter.

Rush: Goodbye, for now.

32

EPILOGUE: IN WITCH EYES OPEN

Gran's house was quieter than ever. Setting foot inside it made me anxious and a little depressed —for multiple reasons.

Part of me still expected to open the door and see feet propped up in Gran's recliner. I no longer had to run and find the remote, gritting my teeth at the sound of the TV— the volume about three times louder than it should be.

But Gran wasn't home.

Summer had taken the cats.

Everything else was the same.

All of her possessions were in disarray, strewn about the house. Her old Buick was leaking oil over the binding circle. I vowed to never use it again.

The stillness gave off a *Sleeping Beauty* vibe. Almost everything about the house gave off a *Sleeping Beauty* vibe.

The stairs creaked under my feet. At the end of the hallway, I found a beautiful, golden-haired woman asleep in my old bed. She hadn't stirred.

My gift had told me more than a dozen times now she was going to be okay. But it hadn't given me a timeline.

My spell was a failure. There was nothing the doctor could do—no procedure for sewing a soul to its body.

He told me it takes time. I had to be patient.

Patience is a virtue Mother Gaia hadn't blessed me with.

I put my palm on my mother's forehead. Her eyes opened at my touch. She smiled at me before closing them again.

Progress.

She was getting stronger.

One day, she'd be able to stand. To talk to me and answer the thousand questions I had for her.

One day, she'd tell me her story.

ACKNOWLEDGMENTS

Thanks to Ellen Campbell who edited this book. To Paula Lester for proofreading. To Jason Gussow for beta reading. And Laura for additional proofs.

Thanks to Jenn for being my amazing partner in this writing journey.

Special thanks to my mother and Don.

As always, thanks to my friends who support me. You're the best!

BY CHRISTINE ZANE THOMAS

Witching Hour starring 40 year old witch Constance Campbell

Book 1: Midlife Curses

Book 2: Never Been Hexed

Book 3: Must Love Charms

Book 4: You've Got Spells

Book 5: As Grimoire as It Gets

Book 6: While You Were Spellbound

Witching Hour: Psychics coming early 2021

Book 1: The Scrying Game

Book 2: The Usual Psychics

Tessa Randolph Cozy Mysteries written with Paula Lester

Grim and Bear It

The Scythe's Secrets

Reap What She Sows

Foodie File Mysteries starring Allie Treadwell

The Salty Taste of Murder

A Choice Cocktail of Death

A Juicy Morsel of Jealousy

The Bitter Bite of Betrayal

Comics and Coffee Case Files starring Kirby Jackson and Gambit

Book 1: Marvels, Mochas, and Murder

Book 2: Lattes and Lies

Book 3: Cold Brew Catastrophe

Book 4: Decaf Deceit

Box Set: Coffee Shop Capers

ABOUT CHRISTINE ZANE THOMAS

Christine Zane Thomas is the pen name of a husband and wife team. A shared love of mystery and sleuths spurred the creation of their own mysterious writer alter-ego.

While not writing, they can be found in northwest Florida with their two children, their dachshund Queenie, and schnauzer Tinker Bell. When not at home, their love of food takes them all around the South. Sometimes they sprinkle in a trip to Disney World. Food and Wine is their favorite season.

Printed in Great Britain
by Amazon